TICKED OFF
And Tickled About It

LOU FINLEY

13 Houses Publishing

THE BIG HUG PAGE

Many thanks to my husband Bob, son Brian,
Daughter-in-law Wendy, grandsons Garett and Kyle.
Every one of them has a great sense of humor.
They keep me laughing.

And thanks to everybody and everything that has
annoyed me. Without you, there would not be
this book.

In memory of my mother Viola and dad Claude
who kept me happy during my childhood.

"WHY IS SHE SO TICKLED ABOUT BEING TICKED OFF," YOU MAY WONDER. HERE'S THE ANSWER....

The great thing about being annoyed, aggravated, angry or madder 'n hell, which all adds up to being "ticked off," is that you recognize there is a problem. If you are the sort of person who thinks, "Oh, there's no problem. Everything will be all right," then you are a person who really, really needs to read this book.

I know there are people who stand ankle deep in a house flooded from a broken pipe and greet the plumber three days after she called him saying, "I'm almost sorry you are here. I haven't had so much fun wading since I was a child." (So I exaggerated a bit.) But the big problem is she calls the same company every time she needs a plumber.

The point is, when something is so wrong that it gets you ticked off, it is time to do something about it. Find a new plumber. Take a college course in plumbing. (If you're not married, it might be a good place to find a nice guy who will be rich one day. Better yet, find a rich, single plumber and flirt your head off.)

Leave the griping to me since I'm going to show you the humor in it. Discard your old ways of whining and crying and look for solutions to your problems. And, please, don't just accept the same problems over and over. But if all else fails, look for the funny side. You will find it here in "Ticked Off and Tickled About It."

Content means happy. This is the **Contents Page.**
(It's where you'll find a lot to make you happy.)

Before the pages (above) there is a Big Hug Page and
a thing about why the author is tickled. Did you
see them? Also------
Don't miss the Thank You page and About the
Author
and then that will be THE END. Thanks for reading.

SOUP TO NUTS

FLAGS ON CUPCAKES

"Flags on cupcakes" has become a slogan in my family. It has to do with what goes on in meaningless meetings. You know, those meetings where you throw up your hands or yawn or start to hyperventilate.

I'll tell you how the "flags on cupcakes" came into being, but I have to digress a little, so don't shout "Flags on cupcakes" yet, please. When my son was in elementary school (a very long time ago), money for workbooks was tight. Sounds just like today, doesn't it? To help out, I volunteered to copy papers for teachers on a mimeograph machine. That was before Xerox machines.

The old mimeo machine was broken more than it was printing and I was the repairperson. (I learned how at one of my summer jobs during college break.)

Anyway, the papers to be copied piled up.

One noon, I went to a PTA meeting in a room next to where I worked. A discussion began about cupcakes that were to be served to the kids for a Presidents' Day party. The question was whether or not to put little American flags that were stuck on toothpicks on the tops of cupcakes.

The discussion went on and on and on and on. Finally I stood up and said, "When you decide whether or not to put flags on the cupcakes, come and get me. I have to mimeograph math books for five teachers."

I left the meeting never to return. I have no idea what happened to the flags on the cupcakes. Frankly, I thought a flag stuck on a pointed toothpick sounded a lot more like a dangerous weapon than a cute decoration. If the kids shouted "Hurray" when they saw them, I suspect it was due to the thoughts they had about where to stick the picks after devouring the cake.

Years later, after the "ah ha" moment just related, I was in real estate sales. At one of our regular meetings of all sales associates, a discussion about nothing of much importance went on way too long. I kept yawning because I was hyperventilating.

After the meeting I told my broker-manager the cupcake story. From then on, he broke up meaningless discussions by saying, "Enough about the flags on cupcakes."

Being the ornery person that I am, I brought a plate of cupcakes to one of our meetings. Yes, they were topped with little American flags and yes the other associates considered using them as weapons on me.

I think big meetings should be a subject for study, but should not be studied in big meetings. Do big meetings ever truly accomplish anything?

When you get right down to brass tacks, decisions are made by a few people within a group. The rest of the hot air blowing around is usually no more important than whether or not to put flags on cupcakes.

My first job out of college was as an advertising copywriter. I spent twenty years in the business and I assure you that great ideas do not come out of meetings between a lot of people. Great ideas come out of one person's head and often out of the blue.

At one point in the 1950's, a large advertising agency decided it would be an innovative idea to put a lot of writers, artists, and account executives into the same room and ask them to come up with ways to sell specific products.

The agency called it "Brainstorming." Braindrain might have been a better word for it.

It didn't take long for Brainstorming to bite the dust with knowledgeable agencies and companies.

Maybe the committees need to be even smaller since the ideas coming out them don't seem too great either.

Can you imagine how many flags-on-cupcakes discussions go on in Washington, D.C.? It boggles the mind!

Here's an idea (from one single person)—Why don't we send every official in the nation's capitol a little American flag stuck on a big cork. Then instead of sticking the flag on a cupcake, they can stick the cork in their mouths. At least until they come up with a really good idea.

WHAT'D HE SAY?

Why is that kids are never just thirsty; they are always "dying" of thirst?

Lee, an eleven-year-old girl, was in my car one hot day and she was moaning, "I'm dying of thirst. I need a soft drink."

Of course, my suggestion, that she drink from the bottle of water I had provided for her, brought on bigger moans. So I drove up to the outside ordering machine of the nearest fast food place.

A voice came out of the air saying, "Face your toter, squeeze."

I've never understood a word that comes out of the speakers. I think it's a secret code that only children can decipher. Even my four-year-old grandson is able to understand the meaning of the strange sounds that come out of the fast food speakers.

It's so embarrassing to have to keep hollering back "What? What? What did you say?" that I never go to those places without a child along.

Anyway, this last time with Lee in the car, the noise coming out of the big ordering box said, "Makel fak rear dorser?

"Yes, please," Lee replied

"Yes?" I wondered. "Are we ordering a rear dorser?"

Somehow Lee completed the order and we drove forward to pick up her drink at the window.

"Floor fallers and flifty pants," the person said. (Are they called tellers or waiters or order takers or clerks? I have no idea.)

I handed my wallet to Lee and said, "You pay him."

"Why?" she asked. (She's eleven. What else is she going to say? Everything is a question about my statements or activities.) Then she added, "Oh, I know, you can't understand what he said. You are pathetic. He said four dollars and fifty cents."

The brilliant comeback I had was, "You're kidding?"

Out of the hole emerged a hand holding two cups and a bag. Apparently Lee ordered more than one drink.

"Here's your lemonade," Lee said. (She knows what I drink before the sun goes down.)

"Check the bag," I said. I have learned that much from my experiences with fast food drive-in restaurants. There is no doubt whatsoever that if you drive off and get too far away to return, you'll find your order missing the main course. Sure enough, the fries were missing.

While waiting for the missing fries, I asked Lee what a hamburger and fries have to do with dying of thirst.

"I forgot to mention that I am also starving."

As the fries and change from my five dollars comes through the magic hole, the waiter, teller, clerk, whatever says, "Hank chew un come (I got that word) gen."

Three minutes later, we were about five hundred miles from that magic hole when Lee says, "Oh, no, we have to go back. There's no ketchup."

"Oh, no, is right," I say, "Because we aren't going back again."

"Well, I can't possibly eat this without ketchup,"
Lee whines. "Oh, look," she says, "there's another
drive-through. We can go in there and tell them they
forgot to give us the ketchup."

"I'll do it, but you understand that we are cheating
and telling a lie. I think the food police will probably
arrest us on our way out."

"Get real," Lee says.

While I'm lecturing Lee on the sins of asking for
ketchup from a place where we didn't buy the food,
she's putting on lip-gloss and brushing her hair.

"Are you going someplace special?" I ask.

"Well, Lee replies, "there's usually a very cute guy at
the pick-up window of this restaurant. I've seen him
here a bunch of times. I'm sure he'll give me the
ketchup."

Since Lee is an especially cute girl, I have no doubt
that she will receive a huge bagful of ketchup. As we
arrived at the window, she said, "Oh, there he is.
He's so cute."

After Lee chatted, smiled, giggled and flipped her
long golden hair around, we drove away with about
20 little packets of ketchup and big smile on Lee's
face.

She was happy as a cat snoozing in the sunshine.

I thought if I could feel like she looks, I'd go to the
drive-through every day. Somehow I would figure
out what the heck "makel fak rear dorser" means.

MUSHROOM SOUP

I am a creative cook. The dishes I create don't
evolve from experience, training, or love of cooking.
They appear out of pure desperation.

The desperation doesn't come from lack of buying
power or living a hundred miles from the nearest
market. We can afford food and are ten minutes
from a huge supermarket.

My desperation comes from a clock, my husband,
and a dislike of any supermarket.

Suddenly in the evening, I'll notice that the clock
shows the time to be way past any reasonable dinner
hour. Or, my husband asks, "Are we eating out
tonight?" Now the ole creative mind has to click in
and fast.

Mushroom soup. I stock up on canned mushroom
soup when I make my semi-annual trip to buy
groceries. (How does anyone survive without
mushroom soup in the house?)

Sweet and sour sauce. I think of that next. I
recently and accidentally discovered sweet and sour
sauce in a can. It was one of my more exciting
gourmet moments. I found this treasure while
searching for the canned mushroom slices. (Now,
don't tell me you can live without those.)

Instant or five minute rice takes up a lot of space on
my shelves, but they are worth it. There are also
instant mashed potatoes sitting there.

If any dish takes longer than five minutes, we'll be eating after our midnight bedtime. Anyway, I have a rule--No meal may take longer than twenty minutes to prepare and no recipe may have more than six ingredients. I stand firm on that last rule.

Cheese. Now there's a food that really brings out my creativity. Cheese on ground meat. Cheese in salads. Cheese on broccoli and cauliflower and beans and bread and potatoes.

Hamburger Helper. There's momma's little helper with a story. I don't use it. But I used to use it. I stopped fixing it the day five friends (former) laughed at me when I said I love it. So, they take cooking lessons. I take writing lessons—I guess so I can write about how I hate to cook.

But I am creative about my cooking. Well, there may be other words for my meal-making talents, but I choose "creative."

The mushroom soup goes over everything—ground turkey, chicken breasts, potatoes and rice. Once I tried the old mushroom-soup-over-green-beans recipe that was a hit at every potluck supper in the 1960's. But the whole country got sick of that.

To add zip, zest and flair to the mushroom soup, I add slices of mushrooms from a can.

So far the sweet and sour sauce has gone over only turkey and chicken breasts. However, this sauce is new in my repertoire.

I admit that I do steal recipes from time to time. I ripped off my mother-in-law's award-winning (awarded by my father-in-law) chopped-up iceberg lettuce mountain topped by a huge piece of chopped steak and the whole thing drowned in homemade chicken gravy.

I was creative because I substituted canned mushroom soup for mom's gravy.

Isn't it wonderful how creative the best chefs can be? When did they start doing what my mother-in-law did years ago and pile one food on top of another?

I'm old enough to remember when the potatoes and rice sat next to the meat, not under it. As kids, we hid the spinach under something else on our plate. Now you find tenderloin steak perched proudly on top of a mound of spinach in the classiest restaurants around.

I also remember when it was revolutionary to be served a dish of food that was decorated with swirls of color or flower blossoms. My mother used to caution me not to eat the flowers in our garden. I did learn that rose petals are very tasty.

Not long ago in a local upscale restaurant, my dinner came with a four-inch tree stuck in the top of the layers of food that made up the main dish. I searched for a tiny bird in the branches but was disappointed not to find anything.

For years I used white dinner plates but then I realized why people loved the colorful Fiesta ware. All food looks more appetizing on colored plates because you can't really see the food.

Next time I have company over for dinner; I may go all out and buy fresh mushrooms to put in the soup.

I'm also thinking that dandelions would look dandy stuck on top of whatever I serve. I have plenty of those prolific little posies in my yard.

If you come to dinner at my house, please BYBAA.

That doesn't mean bring your own liquor. It means bring your own bottle of antacid. I've run out of it and I'm not going to the market for three more months. I'll be out of mushroom soup by then.

COOKIE LOVE STORY

I am a Groupie of the Cookie Monster.

So how could that possibly be annoying? Well, if you'll just give me a chance to finish eating this yummy chocolate chip cookie, I'll tell you all about it.

The problem is—The cookie I just devoured was in a bunch of pieces and crumbles when I rescued it from the cookie bag. (This is a store-bought cookie because if you know anything about me at all, you know I didn't make it.)

No, I'm not ticked off at the store. I am the guilty party. I took the bag out of my pantry and tried to open it. That is somewhat challenging and while wrestling around with the opening, the bag fell to the floor, crushing my cookies.

All right. So what? No, not all right and not so what. I buy the bag of cookies that is as far to the rear of the shelf as I can possibly reach figuring that no fingers have had the chance to crumble my cookies. I carefully place the bag on top of everything in my shopping basket next to the eggs. Both will ride home in my car in the front seat. (Unfortunately they don't make car seats small enough for these guys, but they'll be okay.)

When the supermarket checker is piling my groceries, near the Bagger, as fast as possible, I grab for my cookies and hold them until all else has been thrown in the plastic sack. I gently place them in the bag with the eggs, which I have made sure are in their very own private bag.

Once the cookies get home, they are carefully hidden away from my husband who has to give the secret password to get a cookie. Only one a day is allowed.

So, I'm obsessive about cookies. I know if one of those pesky pollsters asked me what dessert I would vote for in a national bake-off contest, I would have to choose a cookie. Then when asked if I like oatmeal, coconut macaroon, lemon, sugar or whatever, there would be no hesitation to say double chocolate with dark chocolate chips. Well, if you're going to go for it, may as well go for the gold.

By now you're probably thinking that this one of her sillier, more unimportant rants. If so, I'm sorry, but that's how the cookie crumbles.

MILK SHAKE

There was practically a riot this morning at my big local supermarket. Well, maybe three disgruntled women with white hair doesn't qualify as a riot, but we were major annoyed.

Personally, I like supermarkets where I know just where every item can be found. I allow twenty minutes to shop and if I haven't located every item on my list by then, it probably will not be going home with me.

So, I was racing around the market and the last item on my list was milk, but not just any milk, it was for organic milk of a certain brand, which is the only milk my husband drinks.

The supermarket has a very large cold chest of all kinds of milk--soymilk, almond milk, goat milk, chocolate milk. You get the idea. But that is not where they keep the organic milk.

The organic milk has always been located down an aisle with eggs, orange juice, cottage cheese yogurt, etc. It never made sense to me but at least I knew where it was after my initial search some months ago.

Today, it was not in that place. I wasted 22 and a half seconds searching. The Stocker was there moving items around. I said, "I can't seem to locate the organic milk." He said, "It's down there," and pointed to the other end of the store where the cold case of other milk is located. I thought, well they finally put all of the milk in one place.

I trudged down to the milk case and saw everything but the organic milk. Another woman came rushing up to me and said, "It's over there." I turned and saw on an end shelf, the organic milk all by itself. It was where there had always been juice specialties. Only luck would have made me find it without help.

As I'm trudging back down to the area where the milk used to be, another woman said, "That makes me so mad when they move things like that."

I passed the Stocker and said, "Nobody likes where that milk is now."

He very helpfully said, "Okay."

A few years ago, a new company purchased our market. The first thing that happened was, as I'm sure you are guessing, the complete redo of where items were located. It was a very neighborly thing to do because all of the shoppers were getting acquainted as they stopped to ask, "Have you seen what they did with the so and so?"

Never one to keep my mouth shut (surprise!), when I was checking out, I asked the Checker why they didn't provide shoppers with an information sheet about where things were now to be found. He pulled out a sheet beneath the counter and said, "I'll give you this but don't tell anyone because they didn't make them for the customers."

Okay, shall we guess why?

Have you ever heard that there are actual studies about how people shop and how stores can place things, near the checkout usually, that will encourage buying something you don't even want?

That same theory evidently also applies to getting customers to search for things.

For example, I decided I would not buy cookies today. Well, cookies and milk go together so the store would have been smart to put cookies next to the milk. I might have ended up buying cookies and once I got them home, I would have been so happy. I mean if they are here, I have to eat them, don't I?

Maybe you like to wander around the supermarket and search for new goodies. Lots of people do, but I am not one of them.

As I was driving home, I started thinking about change and how as most of us get older, we are not too happy with change. There's the old saying, "He's set in his ways."

Things are pretty stable in my life at the moment so maybe I should celebrate the moments when the milk gets moved to another place. Things like that could shake me up and perhaps that's a good thing.

I used to love milk shakes.

WEIRD NEW WORLD

If the kids who are reading about the strange worlds in Harry Potter books want to find the strangest, weirdest world of all, they need to look in their refrigerator. That is if their refrigerator is anything like mine.

"Mom! Mom! There's something really weird in our refrigerator. It's way cool and so gross." (I wonder how many times I heard that.)

"Dad, the cheese is green and fuzzy. Why don't you ever wrap it when you put it back?"

"I'm not the one who leaves it unwrapped. You are."

"No, I'm not and I'm also not the one who leaves a half a teaspoon of milk in the milk carton. Mom thinks we have milk so she doesn't buy any."

"Mom should shake the carton or open it and peer inside."

"How did I get roped into this war?" I ask.

"It's your fault," they chime in unison.

You think I'm making this up?

And this reminds me that I am the one at fault for everything that goes wrong in our family. That extends beyond husband and son to daughter-in-law now. And with the addition of two grandsons, I fear for my future, but fortunately the boys are still very young.

I have to admit that when I'm blamed, I can't help but laugh because those three are so creative in how they turn something around to make it my fault. If they get desperate, they resort to "Well, if you hadn't married him." Or, "If you hadn't given birth to him."

I thought about all of this when my husband asked me why I don't eat the whole package of baby carrots. Those are the ones that come in little packets for kids to take to school, and then throw in the wastebasket. My husband and I are eating them because we are trying to lose weight. I figure I'll save calories if I don't eat the whole package. I would do that with a chocolate chip cookie but it falls apart when you try to cut it. Oh, well, how many calories could one little cookie have?

But, I meant to rant about the strange things in the refrigerator. How can that mold, bacteria and those peculiar organisms appear so quickly? No one every told me that a refrigerator is just an over-size Petri dish. Ugh!

Sometimes the food is so far gone; I don't know what it was in the first place.

"Mom, look at this." My son was holding a brown shriveled thing that I'm guessing was once a shiny red apple. "I think it's a shrunken head," he says. (Maybe he's right.)

I don't even want to get started on the freezer. It is just full of excitement for the kids. Four-year-old beef patties make great flying saucers. The possibilities are endless.

So, instead of feeling blamed for the state of my refrigerator, I plan to take credit for introducing a whole new world of fun for kids.

So there, Harry Potter.

BAGGED

Odds are there are some kids today who can thank the Bag Boy at my Supermarket for an extra happy Mother's Day dinner. They're the kids who weren't served broccoli or green beans.

I shopped for food to fix my mom a dinner and got a surprise when I unpacked my market bags. There was a big sack of green beans and a large bunch of broccoli. My mom does not like vegetables of any kind. Beans, maybe. Broccoli, no way.

I discovered that I had paid for these little green goodies, but it didn't amount to much. I was concerned that the customer who picked out the veggies would go back to the store and be charged again.

If the customer didn't go back to the store, I'm betting there were some happy kids.

Of course, I can't be sure about that because my four- year-old grandson loves broccoli. He's a unique child, but that might be carrying it too far.

I'm usually the person who doesn't receive all of what I purchased at the market. In fact, this is the first time I have ever, ever, ever gotten someone else's food.

But I've probably trekked back to the store four or five times in the past year to retrieve my groceries. Usually what was left behind was the main course, of course.

We can't blame the Baggers too much for these oversights. I'm pretty sure the supermarkets' training programs consist of handing the Bagger a bag and a can, saying, "Put this into that." There's no time to train because Baggers quit faster than potato chips fly out of the market.

My pet peeve is overly heavy sacks. I ask the Bagger to keep the sacks fairly light as I am not a twenty-year-old weight lifter and I have thirteen steps to climb from my garage to my kitchen. Maybe the ones who speak only Spanish don't understand me when I say, "No mucho." That is about the extent of my Spanish. But, they always smile and nod.

I live in New Mexico and a lot of Baggers don't speak English.

Here's what most Baggers do: They pack all of the bags so they are light, and then they don't fill another bag. They divide up what should be in another bag and put those things into the light bags. That might be okay except what is usually left to divide up are foods such as a huge bunch of bananas, four cantaloupes, a gallon of milk and three six packs of something or other.

(Why start a new bag when there's room in the top of the other bags? That must be what they think.)

Now I need a crane to get the bags up the steps, let alone into the back of my car.

The Baggers at my market are often young men who have worked on their muscles. The best Baggers for me are petite females; they understand the word "light." They even understand when I say "poquito," which I think means "little" in Spanish.

Years ago, one of the very small independent markets had a retired gentleman who helped out doing this and that, but mostly bagging. This man was an artist at what he did. When you left, your food was organized by categories into each bag. No bag was too heavy for a four-year-old to carry. The Bagger insisted on carrying the bags to your car. Of course when this independent market finally had to close its business, there was still a long line waiting to check out. (He was the only Bagger.)

I've always felt that no matter what job you had to do, you should do it to the best of your abilities. Some Bagger may be doing that, but I am pretty sure the vast majority stick the food in the bag and wonder how much longer it is until quitting time. (Actually, I got that information from my husband who was a Bagger in his youth.)

I've figured out how to solve my problem at the supermarket. All I have to do is take up weight-lifting, move to a house without thirteen steps, become fluent in Spanish, try to keep my eye on the Bagger while I'm taking all of my food out of my cart and piling it on the counter and then running my card through the credit machine while making sure I'm pressing all of the right buttons and the correct price is appearing on the screen.

While all of this is going on, the woman behind me is piling her food right behind mine and I can't remember if I saw the Bagger put my chicken into one of my bags or does the chicken on the counter belong to the lady behind? The divider stick has been removed and the clerk keeps asking me to check the charge and push the okay button.

I look at the Bagger, point at myself and ask, "My pollo?"

He smiles and says, "Si."

And you know what? He was right.

EYE OF THE BEHOLDER

DANCING WITHOUT LIPSTICK

I used to be thin. I used to be young. I used to look okay without lipstick. Not anymore.

Somewhere around the age of 70, I decided to start dancing. Everyone says, "What kind of dancing?" I tell them, "It's sort of Fred Astaire-ish, but I can't use his albums because they're too fast. I dance to Tony Bennett sings Fred Astaire." (If you know of anyone who sings slower, email me.)

I dance in front of a big mirror. (That takes a lot of courage.) One day I didn't bother to put on my lipstick. I looked at this pale, old(er) person and said to myself (which is another danger of growing old), "I can't dance without my lipstick."

This whole thing of dancing may sound neurotic to you, and maybe it is. As for me, I began to think about dancing without lipstick and realized I'd hit on a very important philosophical idea. Or, maybe not.

The thing is, I'm trying to hold off this growing old thing. There are telltale signs that the years are moving downhill. The chin drops to the neck. The neck drops to the boobs (assuming you're a gal), and the boobs drop to the navel. The navel does not drop, it pushes out and out. It forms a hill and that's where we get the phrase "going downhill."

All of this is validated by young children. I teach reading to 5, 6, 7 and 8 year olds. They ask, "What is that thing hanging down below your chin?"

I say, "Leave me alone."

I happen to be a redhead (former, now white) with lots of freckles. These are very interesting to the children I work with since most are Hispanic and freckles do not exist in their families. I've heard them exclaim, "Wow, those are really big freckles." I don't bother to show them the difference between freckles and age spots.

Speaking of spots, what are all of those strange things that appear on our skin after the age of ?—well, at least over 65. No one thinks that anyone else has them until they go swimming. Then they realize how lucky or unlucky they are depending upon whether their spots are light or dark. Try to get a dermatologist to remove them without charging an arm and a leg. "They are not important," says the doctor. "To whom?" I ask him as I pay an arm and a leg to get them burned off. (Medicare doesn't think they are important either.)

The figure and the skin aren't the only things to go. Bye-bye hair, down the drain. Men get receding hairlines; women lose hair all over their bodies. The reason, of course, is another loss. The estrogen is gone so we pop pills that are supposed to keep us young. Right!

Back to the dancing. (That's the other thing that happens, as you get older, your mind wanders.) Let's see, what was my point? Oh, yes, you can dance to stay thinner and help your bones to stay thicker, except for one teeny, tiny problem--before your bones get thicker, they, together with your muscles, start to hurt. Now you have to swallow glucosamine as well as estrogen enhancers. This is along with your half of an aspirin per day, and the over-50 multi-vitamins.

Anyway, I was getting my weight down, my bones stronger, my skin problems erased (except for wrinkles), and my blondish hair tri-colored so it would look thicker, and then I got a phone call. Five of my best friends from high school were coming to town for several days. I had not seen these women since graduation. Well, I was feeling pretty good about myself. I figured they would all be fat with thin bones, grey hair and spots on their skin.

The day they arrived, a van drove up. The door opened and out came five thin women without grey in their hair and wearing lipstick. How did this happen?

Well, two of them danced Fred Astaire-style regularly, and slowly. One played tennis--doubles, of course. One was devotee of Pilates; a form of exercise also used by pregnant women nine months along. The other one went to a gym every day, but I have no idea what she did there.

After my friends went back to their homes, I sat down looking into my dancing mirror, wearing my lipstick, thinking about growing old. This is where that philosophy thing comes in.

My wandering mind wandered to this: I no longer have to learn the rules of life as children have to do, struggling to learn my ABC's, forced to sit in a classroom all day. I don't have to worry about boyfriends, because I've been married to my husband for over fifty years. I don't have to get up at 2 AM to feed babies. I have two young grandsons and after I visit, I can leave. I'm retired and choose what I want to do. All of this is possible because I am fortunate enough to be healthy. Dancing helps.

Now, once in a while, I can go without my foundation, mascara and blush without needing psychotherapy. But here's the bottom line, the big Philosophical Rule--Never ever dance without lipstick.

A HAIRY STORY

When my mom was 94, she said, "I'd like some of that stuff I saw advertised on TV that grows in new hair."

This was not wishful thinking on her part; she wanted to try it. It's not like she was bald. Her hair thinned but it looked nice.

"How do I go about getting it?" she asked me, so I knew she was serious.

Since I had just gotten my hair tri-colored to make it look thicker, I was sympathetic. But I hadn't considered doing anything more drastic.

Mom got me to thinking a lot about hair. Obviously I have time on my hands.

I thought about a girl I'd seen with purple and green striped hair. You'd guess she has a wild, flamboyant personality, but maybe she's shy and insecure. Or, how about a grey-haired man with close-cropped hair. He looks like he works for the government, but maybe he's wilder than the teenager's hair looks.

And how neurotic do some men get when their hair starts to recede? I love the comb-it-all-forward look. Then there's the nearly bald guy with the long ponytail down the back. A friend calls it compensation hair.

Take a look at a magazine that features actresses and singers. They want to be unique, but every one of them will have long hair until a star cuts hers; then they'll all have short hair. It's commonly known as the communal copycat hairdo.

Remember the good ole days when we got a hairstyle that was supposed to be personalized for the shape of our face? Beauty magazines had articles about the heart-shaped face, and the oval and the round. No one brought up the triangle or the square. Well, who would?

Teenagers and NBA basketball players top my list of people who dote on their hair. Both groups wear uniforms so they all look like their peers, except for their hair. It's the one way they try to express their own personality. Some personalities appear very scary.

About now you are no doubt thinking, "What in tarnation is she getting at?"

Don't blame me if you don't get it. Blame my mother. She started this hair-brained idea. And as far as I'm concerned, there's really no point except— Hair today, gone tomorrow.

A NEW WRINKLE

When my mother was ninety-four years old, she went to get new eyeglasses. Later that day, she telephoned me and told me about the experience. She said, "I thought I looked pretty good until I got my new eyeglasses."

"You don't like the frames?" I asked.

"They are my same old frames," Mom replied. "The glass is new."

I got her point. Sometimes I take off my glasses, look in the mirror and somehow, I magically grew younger.

Most of us don't see the world 100% clearly without help, and maybe not even then. We may have twenty-twenty vision, but that doesn't mean we see things the way they really are.

Many years ago, I read something in a book about how we see reality. If my memory was twenty-twenty, I would remember the title of the book, but I don't. However, I do remember most of what I read. (Give me credit for something!)

The author of that book suggested an experiment to show how our vision of the world can be so distorted. She suggested looking through an old-fashioned table fan while those dangerous big blades are turning. Then turn off the fan and look past the blades at the same view. You won't see exactly the same thing both times.

And keep your hands to yourself or what you'll be seeing is an emergency room.

There are times when we refuse to remove our rose-colored glasses, preferring to see what we want to see.

At other times, we act like Sherlock Holmes with a magnifying glass, inspecting every little slight and hurt.

And sometimes we see what we see, like it or not, because our eyeglasses have grown weak, or we decide to sit around gazing at a fan, hoping no one will see us doing such a strange activity.

You know who sees things clearly? Children.

Yes, children not only see things clearly, they report it to you in all of its deeply honest details. (Unless they're fibbing to stay out of trouble.)

Kids under the age of eight don't hesitate to ask us about their clear observations. They'll ask, "Why is your face wrinkled? What are those big brown spots on your hands? Why are your teeth yellow? What's that thing hanging under your chin? And under your arms, too?" The biggie: "Are you really old? How old are you?" (Well these are the things I've been asked in the last ten years by the kids I tutor.)

In my opinion, which is what you are being fed here, it gets harder and harder every year to see things clearly, and it's not just because our eyes get weaker.

We're not seeing things more clearly because we are constantly being blinded and broadsided by outside influences such as television, newspapers, radio, email messages, billboards and unsolicited phone calls. Buy this! Do that! Believe this!

You know all of this. We all know all of this. What are we doing about it? We can't get new eyeglasses or turn the table fan on or off to change things in our world.

Recall my mentioning the twenty-twenty memory that's part of our brain? Another part of our brains that rarely gets past 10% use is our reasoning ability. The five letter word expressing it best is…Think, I think.

It seems like too often we do buy into "Buy this! Do that! Believe this!" without giving it much thought.

Those unpleasant little ten second news bites from television that we swallow whole, that slide down the gullet and shoot into the brain should carry warning labels: Caution, Can Cause Blindness to the Truth.

Unless we look hard at all the facts, we won't realize what reality is. Simply stated, we won't see all of the wrinkles.

Mom was blind to the truth of her looks until she got her stronger glasses. And even though she didn't see all of her wrinkles before, she was happier being able to see everything (except her wrinkles) more clearly with her new lenses.

If you prefer smile wrinkles to frown wrinkles, I hope you'll think about my new wrinkle on wrinkles and keep those lenses sparkling clear.

IT'S TOOTH PERFECT

I recently saw Julia Roberts' perfect, gleaming white teeth in the mouth of an eighty-year-old woman.

The sight was startling, especially since those teeth weren't there a year ago.

The woman's teeth were no doubt false, but has the world gone mad with the mania for snow-white teeth? She could have made them a little yellow like the rest of us older folks.

You can hardly watch television anymore without sunglasses. Everyone on TV has spotlights in their mouths. Big, bright, shiny teeth.

Remember in old photos of our ancestors that no one smiled?

My ninety-four-year-old mother said it was because no one wanted to show off their teeth since usually half of the teeth were missing. And they certainly weren't pure white.

My mom watches a lot of television. She said she saw an infomercial where four women, with teeth so white that the glare would blind you, asking a fifth woman how she got her teeth so white. You'd think the other four women would have just a little yellow on their teeth. Why make the rest of us feel bad?

This tooth-whitening craze has swept this country like a blizzard. White everywhere.

When I was a girl, many, many long years ago, it was thought that yellow teeth were stronger than white teeth. (I'm sure someone with yellow teeth started the rumor. The idea caught on since most people did not have teeth the color of a toddler's and wanted to think that at least their teeth were strong.)

I know of four ways a person can whiten teeth today. There's the old standby of toothpaste. But that won't get you to white as snow. Then there's the paint-on whitener. It helps some. There's the wand, which is mostly a variation of the paint-on.

In a class by themselves are the strips. You stick little paper strips of whitener on your teeth, if you can. The bigger the teeth the easier this procedure will be.

Once you manage to get the strips on, you are not supposed to eat or drink. The manufacturer feels the need to warn you. Are they kidding? You can't even talk or the strips fall off.

The fourth method of whitening teeth is performed by a dentist. That will entail the use of a laser or a tray of gunk that sits in your mouth. How long? Too long.

The other day, I bought a tube of toothpaste that is supposed to get you to Julia's white level. (Yes, there are "levels" of white for teeth.) The toothpaste I bought came with a free giveaway of their new product. The product was a whitening wand. Now, I ask you, if the toothpaste is designed to get your teeth to the whitest possible level, why do you now need a magic whitening wand?

Have you gone down the whitening road yet? Well, if you haven't, wait until someone gives you money for Christmas and tells you to use it to whiten your teeth so they'll look like the snow outside the window. (Thanks, Mom!) Or, wait until some kid (kids are so brutally honest) asks you why your teeth are yellow. You'll be down at your local drugstore purchasing a product faster than you can say white, light, bright.

By the way, if you want to talk to me about any of this, don't phone after 10 P.M. That's when I put the whitening strips on my teeth.

A HAPPY MEDIUM

While waiting for my take-out dinners, I read an interview with a "famous" young actress in a women's magazine. (I have no idea who the actress is, since "famous" to me is Lauren Bacall.) Anyway, the actress, who I will call "Tress," was discussing her perfect skin, sparkling eyes and drop-dead figure. She attributed all of this perfection to being a vegan. (No meat for that gal, just lots of tofu-y and soy, grass and grains.)

I was still waiting for my non-vegan chicken take-out, so I read on.

Tress said, "Obtaining my incredible beauty is soooo easy to do, just eat what you want."

"Say what?" I said to myself, peering down at my non-flat stomach, remembering my rather red allergy-inflamed eyes. I couldn't see my skin at the moment, but memory said, "Oh, right!"

What I really wanted to eat were six calorie-loaded chocolate chip cookies. I'd been dieting for about two months (eating lots of no-no protein-laden meat) but the main thing I adore on my menu is chocolate, especially in the form of cookies. I hadn't had a chocolate chip cookie for two months. "Well," I thought, "there we go. I'll eat what I want as Tress suggested and load up on those little goodies."

Doesn't it just burn you up when you hear about some skinny model who tells you she never exercises? My gut feeling (forget the gut!) is a person like that subsists on a peeled grape. However, I bet if you asked her, she would say, "I eat what I want and never gain a pound."

I was still reading the magazine when my chicken with mashed potatoes and gravy and honey-sweeten carrots arrived. I asked for extra bread. It is so good. The restaurant toasts the bread with butter. Now you are thinking, "No wonder she's not thin." Well, excuse me, but do you recall Tress saying that the way to have a stunning body was to eat what you want? Just because all she wants is grass and grains doesn't mean that's what I can deal with.

As I left the restaurant, I glanced at the other customers. Not a skinny body among them, but they all sure looked happy as they devoured the chicken, French fries and bread pudding. And nobody looked like it took a truck and a crane to get him or her there. They looked like a good steak—medium. Well, maybe you like your food rare, but to me that's a little like voting with the skinny group. And well done is a bit over the top.

Personally, I think medium people are too rare and being medium is well done.

Maybe I'll go have a chocolate chip cookie, but just one. That's pretty medium, I think, and I consider medium to be very special.

P.S. I don't want to insult you by thinking that you don't know the definitions of medium, but in the interest of education, here they are: 1. Something occupying a position between extremes. 2. An environment in which something functions and thrives. 3. One thought to have powers to communicate with the dead. (We've got a lot of those Mediums in Santa Fe, New Mexico!)

SNIFFLING AND SNEEZING

You know what I love most about the movie, "You've Got Mail"?

Meg Ryan gets a head cold.

How many other movies have you seen where someone has a cold? I can't recall any. Pneumonia, consumption, flu, of course. But plain ole colds like most of us get at least once a year, never. Movies go for drama. A cold is not dramatic until it turns into pneumonia, etc.

I've got a cold today. My nose is red. I'm on my third box of tissues. Periodically, I have a coughing fit and then my eyes water and my face turns as red as my nose.

Meg Ryan looks cute with a cold.

Trust me, I not only do not look cute, I do not look even half human with this cold. (Even when I was Meg Ryan's age, long ago, I seriously doubt I looked cute with this health issue.)

A cold is supposed to be over and done with in seven days. That's the rule. My doctor verified that seven is the magic number.

Today is my eighth day with this miserable cold and it shows no signs of being gone by the end of the day. Don't tell anyone about this because I don't want to be arrested by the Cold Police for breaking the seven-day law.

Granted, I am feeling much better and maybe by the time day nine dawns, I'll be well. However, on day eight, I am still snooting, sneezing and coughing. I still look like Rudolph the red nose reindeer and frequently sound like a barking dog.

By now, I hope I am gaining a little sympathy from you.

What I have is romantically called "A Summer Cold." I have no idea why the word summer is there. No one ever says, "I have a Winter Cold." But everyone I call on the phone to try and get a little sympathy says, "Oh, Summer Colds are just terrible."

This cold seems just about the same as the colds I've had in the winter. My guess is that Summer Colds have gotten that bad reputation because no one wants to have to stay home for seven days when they could be out playing in the sun.

Staying home is part of the cure, but hardly anyone ever does it and that's why so many of us have colds and have them so often. After all, in case you were just born and don't know, colds are highly contagious.

Another part of the cure is ingesting chicken soup. I now do not care if have chicken soup again for another year. Ordinarily I love this soup. I get it from a local restaurant that specializes in chicken dishes. But after four days of it, two times a day, I would opt for pea soup, which ranks at the bottom of my list of favorite soups.

When I went to the doctor because my throat was really sore, the first question she asked was, "Have you been around young children recently?"

I would have laughed uproariously if my throat hadn't hurt so much. Have I been around young children recently? Yes, indeed. I run a reading program, for children from ages five through eight, three mornings a week in the summer.

This summer, my classes, held in one room, have averaged about forty children each day. They are not always the same children everyday, so I am exposed to about sixty children a week, I would guess. I am so busy working with these kids; I don't have time to count.

I immediately assumed the doctor meant that I had some horrible childhood disease. However, it turns out that this summer, children have had a lot more colds than usual.

I was surprised about this because I hadn't noticed any runny noses and kids are quick to tell me if they don't feel well so that they don't have to learn their alphabet.

Well, if you are reading on hoping that I have a cure for the common cold, you are out of luck. As I've already told you, I just want a little sympathy. Besides as Meg says in the movie, "I'm fuzzy headed." So don't depend on me for answers.

TIRED OF ATTIRES

Have you ever flown for two hours squished into the middle seat of a commercial airplane, seated next to a pair of very hairy male legs? Well, I have, way too many times. Men should not wear shorts when they travel by plane. Period.

My husband, always seated on the aisle, travels in long pants even though he has great legs for shorts. It's a courtesy issue. (Thank you, dear.)

The first time I traveled on a commercial airline, in 1953, I wore a skirt suit with a hat and gloves. So did every other woman on board. So I have now established that, yes, I am from a long ago generation.

I'm sorry but this business of wearing shorts or jeans, tee shirts or sweatshirts, sneakers or hiking boots every single place a person goes really annoys me. Okay, so you're thinking, there she goes again being ticked off over every little thing. But I think it is a reflection of a whole lot more than what you'd see in a mirror.

In this little city of Santa Fe, New Mexico, where I live, jeans and sweatshirts show up at the opera, the ballet and venues with live shows that have ticket prices of $75. I know, that's cheap compared to the big cities, but it's not so cheap here.

A recent invitation to a cocktail party contained an admonishment, "It's casual." Yikes, what does that mean? The event was to be held in a beautiful home so I just couldn't imagine that it meant jeans, sweatshirt and sports shoes (once called sneakers).

I was so puzzled that I looked up the word "casual" in the dictionary. The first definition is: "happening by chance." Another definition is "informal." Under that word is stated: "not according to fixed customs, rules, etc." What customs? I was more confused than ever.

Since I am writing this before attending the cocktail party, I am still in the dark about what "casual" means in terms of an outfit. I'm guessing that it does at least mean clean jeans and no sweatshirts. A fancy tee shirt might work and there are many very fancy ones in the stores these days. Personally, I'm hoping that bodes well for a return to more attractively attired people around here, but I'm not holding my breath.

I visit Los Angeles fairly often and I notice that clean jeans seem to be the "in" thing, but when attending fashionable functions, it does appear that women add high heel shoes and very lovely tops and jackets. Men wear attractive shirts and sometimes even a loose tie and sports coat. I think that is a nice look for this era. But I rarely see it in this area.

Here in Santa Fe, it is a bit hard to go gallivanting about in high heel shoes, as this is not a big city where every inch is covered with concrete. For example, the place where I am going to the party is reached via a gravel driveway. Living on a gravel road here is kind of an upscale thing. Don't ask me why.

"So, what?" you are probably thinking by now. What difference does it make what you wear when you go out on the town (an old saying). Well, whether you like it or not, I am about to tell you what I am thinking.

I think it shows respect for other people to try and look like you care. I think it shows a sense of pride in yourself, which I know is important for a person's own well being. I think a lot of pride in yourself has been lost in this country, unfortunately, and hence (old-fashioned word) too many people no longer take pride in their work or pride in their behavior. I think this lack of pride is one reason for so much rudeness between people.

I'm working on the theory that whistling makes you happy and that you don't have to wait to be happy to whistle. In other words dressing up may actually make you a more delightful person to have around. You don't have to wait until you are delightful to improve your wardrobe.

I realize that many people don't dress up because they want to show that there are much more important things. It's a statement that I am above all this consumerism. Of course there are many people who can't afford as many clothes as other people. And, some young people are just dressing the sloppy way they do to rebel but mature people don't have to dress like teenagers.

The "gently worn" (the definition is "used clothes") stores are filled to capacity now with the economy being such a bust. Everyone wants a bargain. You have to be destitute to go about in tacky, torn clothes. Oh, I know, torn jeans are quite fashionable.

I'll tell you a true story (not one of my infamous exaggerations): Before blue jeans came already distressed, my husband, the clothes horse, tied a pair of brand new jeans to the back bumper of his sports car and drove up and down our double cul-de sac street and then washed them with some bleach.

At this point in this gripe, I am going to stop writing until after I attend the cocktail party. I will then give you a fashion report.

Well, I'm back and have to say that I was very pleasantly surprised. There were no mink coats, diamond necklaces or high heel shoes but there were nice looking jackets, semi-precious stones in a couple of necklaces, and some high fashion boots on the ladies.
The guys were in black jeans, simple trousers, handsome sweaters and shirts.

I have to admit that it was an older crowd, about 55 and up, and either retired from good jobs or still working at something above minimum wage. Money does expand the choices of clothes you can own.

Honestly, walking around the Plaza in Santa Fe in the summer is a fashion show. It is a show of what not to wear. Except for the ladies from Texas. You can spot those gals a mile away. They have been coiffed and made up and outfitted as though the Paparazzi were going to jump out from behind a Russian Sage bush at any moment to photograph their stunning beings. And guaranteed there will be a huge necklace of mostly turquoise draped around the necks. Surely there can be a happy medium of style here somewhere.

Speaking of overdoing it, which is what you are probably thinking about his rant right now, the fashion/cosmetic industry in this country, and the world, is enormous. But really, are we different from the most primitive tribes of way back when? Indians all over the world used face paints and dressed themselves in furs and feathers and jewelry. Do you think any of them would be caught dead in last year's tattered lion fur or bonnet of droopy feathers?

I have to go now and figure out what I'm going to wear to the next party. The invitation said, "Black Tie, Please." It's really nice to be given a hint, but I still have a problem. What do I wear besides the tie?

BITE YOUR TONGUE

WAY TO GO!

The other day I saw a car with bumper stickers that went way above, out and over the bumper. There were stickers with slogans about nearly everything: War, Peace, Water, Environment, Whales, Tuna, Prairie Dogs, Economics, Education, Marriage, and the President of the United States.

No sense to tell you which side they were on, I'm sure you know, and anyway that is not my point.

My point is that it's great we are free, so far, to communicate and have the vehicles to do it. I don't mean just automobiles. I mean we have call-in radio, letters to the editor, standing on the corner with signs, also signs in our yards, and community meetings. This is not even counting demonstrations and marches.

Someone, actually my husband, said, "The problem is, I don't know if doing things like calling, writing, marching and attaching bumper stickers help the causes."

My answer is that it can't hurt and most importantly, taking action makes people feel as though they can make a difference. At least they get to let off a little steam by expressing their opinions.

Obviously, I don't object to expressing myself. I do it all the time in my writings. I also shout back at the bumper stickers, with my windows up, of course. I also talk to the writer of a letter to the editor. Sometimes I say, "Way to go!" Other times I say, "What zoo did you escape from?"

Frankly, I think a museum should have a showing of bumper stickers. Some of them are so creative. (I don't mean, "Nuke the Whales.")

I almost forgot about tee shirts. Today, nearly every tee shirt walking around on someone's chest makes a statement. Not all are political. In fact, ball clubs probably top the list of shirt statements. Last Mother's Day, my kids gave me a tee shirt with the name and emblem of the Lakers basketball team. Go Lakers!

Even little kids' tee shirts sport messages. How about "I Don't Waste Gas. I Ride a Trike"? Or, "Don't Ask My Opinion. I Can't Talk Yet." Another good one for a baby--"I'm a Gas Producer and I Drive People Away."

Babies' bibs have a message as well--"I'm a Little Mess, and Stuff Happens." (Well, I paraphrased that one, okay?)

Who says the individual doesn't have a voice in America? The important thing is to make sure that we always do.

I do know there are a lot of people who don't know how to use their voices and others who are scared to do so. There are still others who should probably keep their mouths shut. Those are the ones who talk first and think later.

I know I'm starting to rant and that's when it's time to change the subject.

Let's talk about baboons and lions and tigers and bears and giraffes and especially about dolphins and whales. All of these guys communicate, but don't you think they would love to have a behind-sticker to glue near their tails, or be able to write a whiny letter to their leader? They just have to grunt and growl and whistle to get a point across. (Of course that is all some of us people do, too.)

I don't have a bumper sticker on my car, but I really admire the owner of the car I saw that had jillions of bumper stickers on the rear end. That person has strong beliefs and is willing to let everyone know what they are. I'd say, "Way to go!" to that driver.

If I had a bumper sticker on my car, here's what it would say—"Stand Up For What You Believe. Never Take It Sitting Down or You'll Have a Pain in the Behind."

KEEP IN TOUCH

Hello, Mr. Hallmark? I'm calling you on my cellphone because this is an emergency. There is a loud disturbance in one of your greeting card stores. I'm standing in it trying to pick out Easter cards for my grandsons. I can't decide between a rabbit card that says, "You had better be a good bunny this year." or one with a picture of a baby chick that reads, "Don't be a chicken next time you see Grandma. Give her a hug."

I might be wrong about what the cards say because there's a woman standing right next to me hollering into her cellphone so I can't concentrate. (Why doesn't someone tell loudmouth people that the cellphone is not a tin can attached to another tin can by a string?)

Anyway, I can't think while this woman is screaming, "Well, he's the one who should be in here buying me the 'I'm sorry' card."

I'm wondering and worrying about the little kid she's mad at. It must be a kid since she's been staring at the children's bunny-chick-egg cards for at least five minutes.

How's your business going, Mr. Hallmark? I remember when people sent cards saying, "I'm thinking of you." Now there's no reason for those cards since everyone is on their cellphone to everyone they know in the whole world. You need to make cards for people to send that say, "Look it's not that I don't like hearing from you, but could you cut it down to once a day instead of every hour?"

I love your cards, Mr. H., but it's hard to get teary-eyed with someone standing next to you shouting, "He's going to get his!" and I don't think this woman means a card.

Apparently this woman is unaware that I'm standing next to her also talking on a cellphone. So here's my idea, Mr. H--I'll try to lead her over to the "I'm sorry" card section across the room. When she finally wakes up to the real world, she won't know where she is since I'm sure she thinks "I'm sorry" is a foreign language.

Okay, Mr. Hallmark, I now have the lady planted in front of the sorry cards and she is still talking (make that shouting) on her cellphone. I believe I have solved my problem so I can go back to the quiet side of the room and pick out the cards for my grandkids. Thanks for your cooperation, Mr. Hallmark, and goodbye.

All right, I exaggerated a bit with the story I just told, but the basics are true. Just consider it a tall tale told to get to a point, which may take even more time to tell.

Before the greeting card incident, I had just returned from a trip to Los Angeles, cellphone capital of the country. (I would say the world, but I understand that title belongs to Tokyo, Japan.) Everyone, I mean everyone from birth to old folks' home is talking on a hand-held cellphone from morning to morning in L.A.

I'm convinced that our next generation will have permanently bent arms with hands that touch the ear just right to cradle a cellphone.

Talk about annoying--no matter whether you are driving or walking around a store, people are on cellphones. If a driver cuts in front of your car, as most of them do, or you miss the green light because the car in front didn't go on the first green light, you can bet the old family home that there's a cellphone stuck to an ear.

Of course the biggest problem is that while a cellphone is in one hand, there's a cup of grande cappuccino from Starbucks in the other one.

I have nothing against cellphones. I own one, which I almost never turn on except to make an emergency phone call to my husband. Well, sometimes a gal just has to ask her husband to stop for take-out on his way home.

I guess I'm old-fashioned and cranky, but I don't understand why cellphones are used so much. When I was first married, in the early 1950's, we didn't even own a phone. We couldn't afford one. I did cheat once in a while and use the public phone in the booth at the corner of my block. That was in the days when there were still public phones and ones that didn't have the cord cut and the coin slots weren't stuck up with gum.

There are lots of good reasons for using a cellphone, but it is pathetic that people can't shop for food without checking in with someone as to whether they should purchase baking potatoes or white potatoes. (I really heard that conversation one day in the produce department.)

It's hard to find something funny about cellphones, but people love them. Even my four-year-old grandson has a toy cellphone. (The toy phone I had as a kid actually was fun because you stuck your finger in a hole and moved a wheel around. What's a toy cellphone do? It just sits there.)

Well, the annoying lady in the Hallmark store finally left. I knew she was gone because I could hear her clear across the store talking to the clerk. I went up to buy my cards and asked the clerk for the address of Mr. Hallmark. I had decided to send him a "Thank You" card.

I found a card with a picture of a cellphone on the front and inside the greeting said, "Thank you. I would have called you, but my cellphone is dead. I would have emailed you, but my computer is in the repair shop. I would have faxed you, but I ran out of paper so I had to send you this stupid greeting card."

When I got back in my car, I used my cellphone to call my husband. I couldn't wait to tell him what had just happened in the greeting card store.

THE SUNDAY PAPER
(Written in 2002 and the facts are facts.)

Every Sunday morning, the New York Times newspaper crashes onto my brick driveway. I'm sure the resounding clunk must awaken the neighbors.

Nearly everybody knows that The Times is the thickest, and so the heaviest, Sunday paper published. It is designed to require at least four to five hours of reading. It's meant to take over your entire morning, or if you go to church, your entire afternoon.

My local paper in Santa Fe, New Mexico, weighs in a whole lot lighter than The Times. I'm used to the big Los Angeles paper on Sunday mornings but I'd have to wait days for it to get here. The New York Times is thrown right on my driveway together with my local newspaper. But only on Sunday.

A big ole Sunday paper is just so much fun.

William Safire has a regular column "On Language" in the New York Times magazine section. It will take me the five hours to understand that one page article. It's so erudite (catch that word?) that I get about one-fourth of the way through and have to start over. What did I just read? What was he saying?

The New York Times does not talk down to its readers. At least not to this reader.

Not that there aren't frivolous articles. Today there is a half page spread about 300 drag queens arriving by ferryboat on Fire Island. It seems this is the 28th year of the so-called "invasion." I hope this isn't considered a serious article.

Then there was a story on the reported "Death of Couture." It seems death was exaggerated and haute couture is still hot. Perhaps the rumor started because less than 500 suits priced at $35,000 each are now sold. It didn't say how many used to be sold, but evidently this is a big dwindle (or is a swindle) and therefore a big story. No doubt by now you are beside yourself with grief. Really, was it essential this information be published? Maybe the death should have appeared in the obituary section.

Now I know you needed to know this fact--The museums in New York City are "suffering from identity crises." How do you get one of those huge things on a psychiatrist's couch? To be real honest, it sounds like a very serious situation and one that may require more than Valium. It sounds like a hefty dose of cash is needed.

Upon reading the book section, I was bereft to discover that "The Farting Dog," a children's book, has finally fallen from the top ten books. It has been replaced by "Cheater Pants" and "Toothless Wonder" among others.

When I come to the technology section, I don't hang around long. I really don't care about a power cable modem that needs a router but first requires a high-speed connection, or maybe a power-line bridge. This all seems to have something to do with Broadband, whatever that is. (Remember this happened in 2002. We've come a long way, baby!)

Now you may believe that money doesn't buy happiness, but you are wrong. This is according to a new "rigorous econometric analysis." It states that money does buy more happiness. It seems there is a new fast-growing field called "happiness economics."

Happiness economics applies to "econometric techniques, traditionally limited to matters like wage rate, to the amorphous arena of human emotion."

I'd better get back to William Safire. I'm starting to understand what he's trying to say.

Before I locate William, I turn a page and am hit with the sight of nine sets of teeth. These belong to past and the more recent presidents. I thought it was an ad for tooth whitener, but I realized some (many) were befores instead of afters.

The article is about whether or not looking good helps to get a guy elected President of the United States. The answer was, of course, it depends. It seems you can look too good. Expensive haircuts, for example, have been known to drop the approval rating.

Of course, for a lot of people, the only really important reason for buying The Times is to get the crossword puzzle and acrostic. Personally, I don't do them. When I see things like "51 Euclidean subj.," I hustle right back to Mr. Safire. I've only spent four hours on his article so far. Maybe I'll get it in five.

That would call for a high five!

A MOVING MOUTH

My youngest grandson has a mouth that's part of a head that never stops turning, arms that never stop waving, and feet that constantly wiggle. All the while he's bouncing up and down. (The whole family is terrified to face the day he starts walking. Already his parents call him "Train Wreck"*.)

The moving mouth also emits every sound known (and unknown) to man, with rare silences. Most of the sounds relate to unbridled joy. Thank goodness.

While trying to get a spoonful of mixed-up cauliflower and spinach (ugh!) to *T.W.'s mouth, I realized the mouth is directly attached to his eyes.

Up goes the closed mouth as the eyes take in the fascinating acoustic ceiling tiles. I take aim for the mouth as it starts to open; the eyes look for Daddy. Food enters his ear.

"Where did that very big, funny, comfortable daddy go?" or so he appears to think as his eyes and head roll this way and that.

"Oh, there's the one called 'mommy'." T.W. begins to laugh and wave his arms even faster, resembling hummingbird wings in flight. (The wings clearly belong to his baby-bird mouth that I am still trying to feed.)

As I watch T.W. wondering what thoughts are going through his developing mind, I think of Irish, our Golden Retriever dog. My husband and I are always trying to figure out what he's thinking.

Before we left to visit T.W. and G. (our other grandson), my husband took our dog to "summer camp." (This is our name for the wonderful no-cage kennel where we board Irish.)

Once we were on our way to California, my husband and I began to wonder what the dog was thinking about being dropped off again at the kennel. He did have immediate separation anxiety, lowering his tail and looking apprehensive. We decided that he was thinking, "I've been a good little boy so why have they gone away? Oh, boy, look at all the dogs I can play with. Woof. Woof."

Do you know anyone who doesn't make up what a baby or puppy is thinking?

In the photo album of my son's baby pictures, under each photo, I wrote what I thought he was thinking. The comments are very creative such as, "Oh, looky, looky, there my big red ball."

Well, I tried.

We visited some former neighbors in California and they don't have any grandchildren. They showed us photos of the birthday party they gave for their sixteen-year-old dog. They told us that he loved the party and especially liked opening his presents. I hope they do a photo album and write under each picture just what they think the dog was thinking. It would be wonderful.

Putting words in the mouths of babies and animals is not only fun, it's necessary since they can't communicate the way adult humans do.

But, second-guessing an adult is not the same as thinking you know what a baby is thinking. Judging what an adult is thinking, without asking, is like aiming for an open mouth but ending up sticking it in an ear. It's messy and doesn't get you where you wish to go. But of course, you know that.

Cauliflower and spinach baby food is bad enough to clean up, but adult messes are usually a whole lot worse. The photo caption might read, "Oh, looky, looky, that used to be my best friend, but not any more."

So I'm going to stick to thinking that "da da" means "daddy" and (my thought) that "goo goo" means "Good grandma." I leave "woof woof" up to you.

SHRUG VS. SORRY

Remember when gasoline stations were called service stations? Unless you're as old as I am, you probably don't remember. But where you went, back in the good ole days to fill your car with gasoline, there were real people to pump the gas and wash your windshield and even check your tires. No charge except for the gas. Most of the time, the service person would even look you in the eyes and smile. I believe there was a gasoline company with the slogan "Service with A Smile."

Now what you get at most gasoline stations when the machine doesn't work properly is not an apology (sorry), but rather a movement of the body called a shrug. The shoulders go up and corners of the mouth move down. Not yours. Theirs.

This motion is known as the so-what shrug. This particular shrug graphically says, "I am NOT contrite, repentant, remorseful or regretful; I am not going to apologize for your inconvenience."

There are shrugs that indicate, "I don't know," but the corners of the mouth don't usually droop. And maybe you use the shrug for other expressions. However my concern is about the shrug that replaces an apology, the one indicating that a person doesn't give a flying leap about what happened.

Of course, the word sorry doesn't always convey the feeling it should. A person may use a certain tone of voice that tells you saying the word is just something that has to be done. To experience sorry in this manner, listen to a child, who is told by an adult to say, "I'm sorry." The sincerity of the apology will often be graded poor because the kid turns around and does the same unacceptable action again.

So do adults.

What has happened to the lack of verbal apologizing for doing a wrong? The lack of this action is seen everywhere in the shrug and heard daily in the form of excuses.

My recent experience was with a clerk in the mini-market attached to a gasoline station. When the "Yes" button on the fill-er-up machine failed to produce my receipt, even though I pushed the button twice, I got a message reading "go inside."

When I saw the clerk, I said, "Is the machine broken? It didn't give me a receipt."

He replied, "No, it's your fault because you didn't push the button."

This over-the-top line was concluded with the classic so-what shrug as he looked at me with a down-turned mouth and handed me a receipt marked "Duplicate" at the top. He then resumed reading the morning newspaper.

I turned and left, fuming worse than gasoline smells.

Saying sorry has apparently gone on a long vacation with thank you and please.

I wonder where those polite words are hanging out these days. Certainly not in most stores, schools, homes or even in Washington, D.C.

We should send out the Apology-Words Police to search for them. We really need to find these polite little guys because without them, people are becoming more and more angry at each other.

Saying "I'm so sorry," can be very soothing to someone. On the other hand, the so-what shrug is infuriating. "So what!" made it all the way to the mouth of a former Vice President. It's time to vote those two words out of our language.

But if you ask me what we can do about this, I would just have to give you the I-don't-know shrug. I'm sorry.

A HOLDUP

I've been held captive in my own home for hours while forced to listen to boring music and annoying sales pitches. The experience is known as being On Hold. That's what the captors call it. I think it's more like a Holdup.

You've waited during the phone calls for necessary service where you are forced to hold on way too long to speak to a live person. Is there anyone in this country who hasn't been On Hold?

Trying to get hold of someone to fix your non-functioning phone or your television or your alarm system or any number of problems can be one of the most frustrating times in your day. And it can certainly use up a lot of hours in your busy life.

One of the most aggravating On Hold calls I've ever encountered involved my home security system.

The alarm company dispatched police to my home because there was an alert signal from a motion detector and I wasn't home. "Change the battery," the alarm company advised.

My husband and I have changed lots of smoke alarm batteries over the years but never a motion detector. We still haven't changed one because when we took off the cover, the inside looked like something dreamed up by NASA. This was the reason I had to make a second phone call to the alarm company. I set up an appointment for a repairman. He discovered the problem was not the motion detector. It was an outside door battery.

Both times I called the alarm company, I was On Hold for over twenty minutes. A recorded voice came on every two minutes to say, "Your wait time will be greater than two minutes." (Excuse me?)

In the twenty minutes of waiting, that meant that I heard that irritating voice ten times. The voice would interrupt the multiple recorded sales pitches, which mainly touted the greatness of the company's service.

I would have thrown my telephone through my office window, but that would entail a call to the phone company and one to a glass place.

I considered sending a bill to the company for the cost of my time. However, since I am retired, I couldn't figure out what I'm worth. Maybe if those of you who get a paycheck would bill these companies for your time, they would get the point. On the other hand, they would probably ignore the bill.

Since you often can't change to another company for service, as it is a monopoly, you really are held captive.

I told you--Hold On is a Holdup.

I was born in the 1930's and there was no Hold On when you phoned a company. Not for years. There were live people with smiles in their voices to say, "May I help you?" and mean it. They answered the phone right away. It was a matter of pride and courtesy to give good service.

I do write complaint letters. I also write letters when the service is especially good. As for my alarm company, I have a choice and I am switching. No Holdover for this gal.

I say arrest the Holdups of Hold Ons.

OUT OF THE MOUTHS OF BABES

WHAT'S A WHOPPER?

Years ago, we had a cat named Armstrong. It was the cat that our young son would blame if his pants accidentally got torn or his milk spilled or a half-eaten apple was left in the refrigerator. "Armstrong did it," he'd say and then laugh because he knew that we knew it was a joke.

One day, I read a story to my class of first and second graders about a pair of gloves that talked to one another. Afterward, I asked the kids what they thought about the story. One eight-year-old boy folded his arms, leaned back in this chair, looked at the ceiling and said, "I don't believe a word of it."

When I asked him why he didn't believe it, he said, "Gloves can't talk."

The seven year old next to him threw up his arms, looked at the boy who had just spoken and shouted, with great disgust, "Imagination! Imagination!"

I asked the questioning youngster, "What about all of those animal books we've read where the bear talks to the lion and so forth? You've never complained about them, have you? Do you really think the bear and lion speak English?

When I worked with children on writing poetry, they had a lot of trouble understanding the difference between truth, imagination, lies, and even jokes in the poems. It takes experience to be able to differentiate.

The wishes and dreams didn't cause many problems, but the children struggled to understand about other made-up ideas. The kids wondered why they weren't lies if they weren't true. And they knew they shouldn't tell lies.

I suggested the class write a poem about lies. When I asked one young girl, "What is a lie?" she said, "A lie is a worm in the apple." She was five years old. "Out of the mouth's of babes" as the old saying goes. I was so astonished that I never questioned her further.

The word lie is being heard a lot from the grownups who are in charge of our country, and the ones who want to be. They're trying to put a spin on the issues of the day, and long ago, such "spins" were called "whoppers" or "tall tales," but people understood that what was being told was not true. Too many adults today don't seem to get that most of today's spins are simply lies.

Maybe things would be better if everyone understood what it means, "A lie is a worm in the apple."

DOLLS' WEDDING

I've been playing with dolls lately even though I'm way into my 70's and even though I didn't like playing with dolls when I was a little girl. But don't call out the men in white coats yet because there is a reason for this activity.

I am a big Sister* and my Little Sister is eleven years old. She's also the greatest Little there has ever been. I've watched her grow up since she was seven.

My Little Sister (I'll call her "L".) and I have done every kid-friendly thing there is to do in this town. At least I thought so until recently.

L and I had never played dolls together. Don't knock it if you haven't done it. You will return happily to the best days of your childhood.

L hauled out two beanie kitty cats, scissors, thread, a doctor's kit, a box, and assorted pieces of material. The cats arrived in the same box, side by side, with a tiny blanket over them. There was a lid on the box. L informed me that it was time for the girl and boy cats to get married.

She had made a little costume for the boy cat some days before and it was too small for him. So, she performed an operation and I stood by as the nurse. L proceeded to make an incision in boy cat's tummy and let the beanies spill out all over the table and floor. When she felt that he was thin enough for his clothes, she sewed him up. I held the paper oxygen cup over his nose.

After the cats were appropriately dressed, the box was covered in white and all of the teddy bears sat around except the green teddy. He performed the ceremony.

I'm telling you, I was almost in tears. It was a beautiful wedding. The honeymoon destination was kept a secret.

If you don't have a girl to play dolls with or a little boy to share his cars, you are missing out on wonderful moments in your life. You know where to find them. I told you where I found L. There are lots of children that would love to read to you or allow you to help them with their homework as well as just play.

You're never too old to pretend to be young.

*Big Brothers/Big Sisters is a National Organization.

KIDDIE BEDLAM

Children could learn to read more quickly if they didn't have to go to the bathroom.

I conduct an after-school program for beginning readers and sometimes we (myself and other volunteers) find time to actually teach.

Much of the class time, however, we have interruptions.

Before we can get the class started we have to get the kids to sit and be quiet so we can't be interrupted.

My puppy learned to sit faster than these kids.

"Be quiet" is apparently a foreign language to these youngsters.

Once we get started with lessons or reading, everyone has to have a drink of water. Right now.

Liquid refreshment time over, each child has a very important pronouncement to deliver, at top volume, to a neighbor.

"But I just had to tell him…blah, blah, blah."

"BE QUIET," I shout over the noise.

"Teacher, I need a pencil."

There's a big container of pencils sitting in the middle of every table.

Okay, we're underway. Everyone has what is needed to work.

"Teacher, I have to go to the bathroom. Bad!"

"Me, too."

"Me, too. I can't wait."

"Me either."

The words "me, too" echo around the room.

"Teacher, my dog had puppies yesterday. They are blah, blah, blah."

"That's great," I tell Felix. "Now, QUIET!"

"Teacher, how many more minutes until we go?"

"A lot. Get to work."

(Did I mention that this class is only 45 minutes long?)

"Teacher, I don't understand what this sentence means."

"Teacher, what's this word?"

"Teacher, it's raining."

Every child immediately runs to the window. Rain and snow are great excuses for not working.

We know these kids are creative because they come up with excuses for leaving the room that none of the grownups would have ever considered: I have to go tell my older brother something. My mother said I don't have to be in here. I can't be in here because I was in an auto accident. ("My, I say, were you hurt?" The answer is "no" and further questioning establishes that the accident was many days ago. I swear this is true.)

Finally we near the end of the class and cleanup time.

This takes about ten minutes.

So the children have received about fifteen minutes of reading instruction and about fifteen minutes of instruction on sitting, working, being quiet, and how to clean up the room. The other fifteen minutes, at least, went for drinking water, their questions, and going to the bathroom.

The teachers, on the other hand, got a full forty-five minutes of practice in dealing with bedlam.

And you know what--We teachers can't wait to do it again.

OH, NO, NO PHOTO

I received a photo from 800 miles away--a picture of my three-year-old grandson. He had a finger up his nose.

"What a precious moment," I thought. "Think of the joy I'd miss if it weren't for a digital camera and a computer."

When my son was growing up (starting in 1964), we had a camera. Sometimes we had photos from that camera. Often we did not. I have very few photos of my son's Birthday parties or of Christmas under the tree. We took them; we just didn't get the film out of the camera in a way that would allow printing. Most of the time we forgot to rewind the film before removing it. My son feels he was a photo-deprived child.

For example, for my son's fourth Birthday, he received Scarletina. That was not a gift from Italy. I discovered little red splotches on his tummy when I gave him a bath on the morning of his party. Not exactly what you want to print and save. By the time he recovered, his day of birth was long gone. But even without a photo, all of our family remembers the day—vividly! And we remember that there was no party.

Another Birthday (in late January in Los Angeles) the rain poured and poured. We lived in the hills, which were rapidly washing down to the valley. It was not a day for a party. By the time the mud was cleared away that Birthday, too, was long gone. We took pictures of the mud but forgot to rewind before removing the film. (Makes us sound pretty duh, doesn't it?) Anyway we didn't need the pictures because all of our family and friends recall filling hundreds of bags of mud that day. (Some of our friends are still speaking to us.)

Then there was the never-to-be-forgotten eighth Birthday. I chose to have the party at a nearby hotel because my husband had been in the hospital. He was at home recuperating. I was sure it would be easier to go to the hotel. (Boy, was I wrong.)

I booked a young magician to entertain the kids. What a mistake and what a nightmare.

One of the young guests, also an eight-year-old boy, sat in the front row and never shut up.

"I can do that. I know how that's done. Oh, that's easy. That's a dumb trick."

On and on he went. We couldn't get him quiet and the magician was getting flustered and annoyed. Fortunately, the pictures I took of an angry-looking magician, a maniac kid and a sad Birthday boy ripped as I took out the film. It hadn't been rewound. We'll never forget that party either. Just ask my son.

By now, I'm sure you've already guessed my message --I don't always need photos. I remember those special times. They're called memories, often more clear and beautiful than any photo could possibly be. And sometimes not so beautiful, but to be cherished nevertheless.

Memories should be held onto because photos may fade or get shuffled into a big box, never to appear again. I hope I never lose my memories.

But there are times when only photos will do.

How else could I see that one treasured moment when my handsome little grandson had his finger up his nose?

LEFTOVER TISSUES

I've finally solved the problem associated with the pocket size facial (nose) tissues. Oh, you didn't know that there is a problem? Well, I have annoying sinuses. (No, this is not a health article.) If I go out of my house, one of those packets always goes with me.

The problem arises when I'm left with one to three tissues and I'm leaving for the day. I need a full pack. So the leftovers end up in a big cardboard box and that's where they stayed until I figured out what to do with them.

When I began teaching a reading program after school to five through eight-year-old children, I took the leftovers to class. That's how I solved my problem.

The kids just help themselves and we no longer have drippy noses around us. They consider being able to go get a tissue for themselves to be a treat.

I put a bunch of packets into a large see-through plastic bag. Every packet is alike, but a child will search the bag looking for one more special than another. Mine came in different colors on the packaging.

The children I work with are from families without much money so treats get the kids excited. The treats are nothing big: Five pennies for winning a word bingo game, red stars drawn on the board for being extra good, a small package of chewing gum, or one small piece of candy, sugar-free. Being the child that gets to hand out the treat at the end of the class is a big treat even though every child gets a turn.

But the best treat of all is the one you'll probably find hard to believe. The kids love to be able to go to the cupboard and pick out the book they want to read, not one they're told they must read. Most of the time they don't pick a book that's considered easy to read; they choose one that is over their heads.

Every child that's been in my class in the past ten or so years has told me that he or she can read. Some can't even write the alphabet, but they're certain that they can read. They also believe in Santa Claus.

But somewhere along the line, too many children stop believing in Santa and a lot of them stop believing they can read every book. They often stop believing in their abilities and that treats lay ahead for them. They lose hope unless we give it to them.

I know, I'm supposed to be writing about being ticked off, and I am.

I'm ticked off that so many children don't get the help they need. And when it comes to the needs of children not being met, I just can't find the humor.

But I know where to find a tissue--for the tears I shed.

SNEAKER CITY

I was looking around in an upscale furniture store the other day when I spotted something really unusual. The saleslady was wearing four-inch high heel shoes.

"So?" you say.

Well, this is not New York City. I live in the little city of Santa Fe, New Mexico.

If you wear high heel shoes here, you're just courting the disaster of a broken ankle, leg or some other body part.

Santa Fe does have a few sidewalks but they are mostly left over from the days of cobblestones. The more modern ones apparently date back to the discovery of concrete. Walking around here requires eyes down, not eyes front.

Santa Fe is THE city of flat shoes. Anyone wearing another kind of shoe is suspected of actually working somewhere, like a bank. The people in cowboy boots are tourists. They're probably wearing the boots for the first time, having confused New Mexico with Texas.

(No one ever knows where New Mexico is, anyway. It's the place on the TV weather map behind where the weather girl or guy always stands.)

Nowhere are sport shoes, which I still call sneakers, more colorful than at places where children congregate.

I work with elementary school children at the local Boys and Girls Club. It's a great place to watch the sneaker parade.

The youngest girls have sneakers in pink and purple with little flower designs and glittery objects attached. Sometimes the sneakers have inlays of shiny silver or gold material. Because the five and six-year-olds don't know how to tie their shoes or else they can't be bothered, most of the girls have sneakers with Velcro flaps or with zippers.

The younger boys prefer sneakers with lots of hot colors. Bright red, orange and blue are in many combinations. The main thing I notice about the boys' sneakers is the condition. Their sneakers have seen a lot of ball kicking, floor scuffing and playing in the dirt. Some of the boys can't tie their shoes either, but they wouldn't be caught dead with zippers on their sneakers. Velcro flaps, rarely. So their sneakers have long, trailing shoelaces. Triple knots don't seem to help matters much. I have re-tied laces I previously knotted three times.

The girls' laces are usually fairly clean and in pastel colors while the boys' are so dirty that even the black is brown.

While the girls' sneakers are pretty, they don't have the character of the boys'. Besides the accumulation of dirt on the boys' shoes, and the scrapes and dents, there are the wrinkles. I can see how they get wrinkled across the kids' toes, but it took me a while to figure out how the creases came across the heels. Mainly it's because the boys are in too big a hurry to get their feet all the way into their shoes. Then, too, it's a lot of fun to step on the back of each other's sneakers—the old flat-tire trick.

About the lady in the high heel shoes, I'll bet she goes home at the end of the day and puts on sneakers. After all, she's living in the city of sneakers.

My question now is…how did people walk around
on the cobblestones here before the age of sneakers?
They must have hobbled over the cobbles.

FLOTSAM AND JETSAM

MEOW AND YEOW

I was thinking about our country's "War on Terror" when I recalled the antics of three cats that once let my family share their home.

There was a grey male cat, a blonde female cat, and a brunette female cat.

The male cat was much larger than the other two but not aggressive. He just wanted to be left alone to eat, sleep and try to sneak out of the house.

The blonde cat was the male's girlfriend until my son conducted their marriage, complete with bridal veil and flowers.

After the wedding, the bride frequently bopped her husband on his nose—for no apparent reason.

As soon as the male let out a YEOW, the brunette cat hurried to give him a hard right to the nose. Who knows why, but there was no sympathy from that gal. In fact, she always followed through by picking a fight with the blonde kitty.

Once Ms. Brunette finished fighting, the blonde cat would slap her husband again.

I believe this is considered escalation. (It probably also caused alienation of affection.)

Sorry to say, these antics used to make us laugh, especially the part where the brunette swung her paw at the nose of the male, who was already the injured party.

No wonder the poor ole guy was always trying to sneak out of the house.

I would not classify the actions of my cats as civilized even though they had their own feline social order. These little animals showed no compassion. I will go on to say that they interacted exactly the way too many humans do.

Who knows what the male cat did to incite the blonde female. Maybe he had stolen one of her kibbles. She'd pick a fight when he seemed to be doing nothing more than sleeping near the heater, minding his own dreams.

The point is, did she lay down with him and try to meow it over? Did they communicate or did she just decide to give him a yeow-up call?

Mr. Male did not strike back. He simply let out a YEOW that said, "You hurt my nose."

It seemed that Ms. Brunette thought, "He has no right to disturb my sleep with his big ole YEOW." So she got into the action and smacked him. Bop! Bop!

Now what would have happened if Mrs. Blondie had awakened her hubby with a nice lick all over his face instead of a bop? Would that have been so bad? Of course, this would not be the "I'm gonna get 'em," approach. Even Miss I-Can't-Wait-to-Slap-Them-Both Brunette would have only purred in her sleep. There would have been no YEOW to disturb her nap.

Just a thought.

My other thought is that the actions of this country have awakened sleeping cats everywhere and YEOWS are going to continue to escalate.

So what I'd like to know is--Whatever happened to encouraging meows instead of YEOWS?

OPEN OTHER END

The day we become eighteen, the shout goes up, "I'm free. I'm free." We think we won't have to take orders from anyone ever again. Oh, sure, we know we're not supposed to speed, run red lights or spit on the sidewalk. (Well, that's an old-fashioned concept!)

And, you may not have thought about a whole lot of other restrictions you face.

How about these orders: Open Other End. Next Line, Please. Use Other Door. Do Not Shake. Enter Here. Push. Pull. Exit. Enter.

Do you consider these to be instructions? Think about it. What happens if you disobey? They sound like orders to me.

What on earth made me think of orders versus instructions? Answer: Toothpaste.

I started to open a new toothpaste box at the wrong end. It said so on the box. "Open Other End," the flap stated.

My hand stopped moving immediately and I whined, to the box, "Oh, I'm so sorry. I didn't mean to do the wrong thing." Then I opened the other end. I looked over the tube and box very carefully to see what dire consequences would have occurred if I had said, "Bite me" and opened the opposite end.

Ah ha! If I hadn't opened the correct end, I would have missed seeing a paper explaining what a wonderful job the toothpaste would do in keeping teeth cavity-free and sparkling. Why would I need that paper? I had bought the particular toothpaste because I already believe it is the best.

Imagine if I had taken the tube of toothpaste out of the box bottom first? Horrors! We're not talking about the delivery of a baby here. It is not, I realized, life-threatening if the bottom of the tube comes out before the cap.

I wonder if there are Toothpaste or Box Police to arrest us for misbehaving when we open the wrong flap. (Does this fall under the Patriot Act?)

There are a lot of subtle orders, rules, or whatever you want to call them that we sometimes invent for ourselves. For example, when my husband and I retired, we were free to eat dinner at any hour we chose. But when it came time to stir up a meal about 5:30 (instead of 7 or 8 o'clock as we had to do for years), my husband said, "Do you think it's okay if we eat this early?" Being the smart mouth that I can be, I said, "We'll be very quiet about it so the Food Police don't get us." (Come to think of it, I wonder if Big Brother has his eye on our dinner rituals.)

Freedom means being free, so what does free mean? We need to look up the meaning of the word free in the dictionary. Otherwise we won't know what we're talking about.

The first definition in my dictionary is: …not under the control or power of another. The fifth meaning is …not confined to the usual rules. The tenth meaning is enlightening; it is…exempt from taxes, duties, etc.

Based on these three meanings, it is doubtful that anyone on earth is truly free.

The word freedom has been freely tossed around in speeches. In the 2005 Inaugural Address given by the United States President, for example, the press reported that the words freedom and/or liberty were used forty-nine times.

The second definition of freedom is: …having civil and political liberty. Now we're getting somewhere because the first definition of liberty is…freedom from slavery and captivity.

So, when we turn eighteen, we should be shouting, "I'm liberated. I'm liberated." because all we are becoming free of is having to be home by certain hours, otherwise known as captivity, or free to say, "I don't want to do the dishes or clean my room," which anyone under eighteen considers slavery.

Freedom and liberty are what we call "big words," not because they have lots of letters in them, but because the meanings encompass so many important ideas not to mention the intense emotions and actions the use of the two words stir up.

Thinking about freedom and liberty wear me out, and besides I have to go brush my teeth. By the way, I checked the toothpaste tube to see if it said, "Do not squeeze in the middle," but I'm home free on that. I can squeeze it anywhere I like because there are no laws printed on the box.

So at least dental squeeze-wise, it seems I'm liberated. Still, those toothpaste boxes are downright dictatorial.

STUCK ON STICKERS

I picked up a bottle of over-the-counter medicine at my friendly neighborhood drugstore and tried to read the label. Usually the print on the label is so small you need a telescope to read it since a magnifying glass is not powerful enough.

It just so happened that I had a pair of brand new lenses in my glasses and could see the print just fine, thank you very much. However over the part that warns of the four hundred and fifty million hideous symptoms the medication could cause, there was a price label from the store.

I was able to see the big red word "IMPORTANT" and below the label was printed "or you could die a horrible death." I imagine the warning included the instruction to not take the entire bottle at one time, but that's just a guess.

At this point do I need to tell you that I have two major faults? One is that I tend to exaggerate and the other is I rarely admit that I exaggerate. But I'm going to come clean and tell you that I did fib just a bit about what the label stated. However, price label cover-ups happen much too often and that's my gripe.

Go into a bookstore (if you can find one that's still in business) and try to read what the book you're holding is about. No way. There will be a price sticker right smack dab in the middle of that information. Or maybe you were the one in sixty zillion who saw what this book is about before you bought it. If so, you can skip being ticked off this time.

There is always room for the price sticker to be placed where it does not interfere with the important words on a product. So why, I wonder, isn't that the place where the sticker sticks?

My theory is very simple: The Sticker (person) of the sticker is not stuck on the idea of serving the customer. The Sticker has a hand-held machine that plops the price sticker very rapidly onto whatever surface the glue touches. The Sticker's goal is to get those little pieces of paper onto the object as quickly as possible so the Sticker won't be late for coffee break or lunch or quitting time.

But really, I don't blame the Sticker. The Sticker has a boss who has a boss who is the CEO of the corporation. The head honcho sends a memo stringing its way down the chain of command. The memo says, "The sticking of the price stickers must be accomplished in an expedient way by the Sticker." In other words, shake a leg because time is money and money comes before serving the customer.

Perhaps you feel this is a very minor subject to get so irate about. However, do you realize that we are being refused vital information? Well, it's not always a complete cover-up. Sometimes we can remove the sticker. Of course that has to be done after purchasing the product or we'll be stuck in jail for tampering. Also some stickers peel off and others require a crowbar. (I warned you that I exaggerate.)

This gripe is one of those waste-of-time gripes because there is not a chance that the Sticker's boss is going to say, "Take your time putting the stickers on the product; we don't care how much it costs the company. The important thing is to give good customer service and to make sure the customer knows the truth."

Can you imagine calling the Customer Service Department or store manager and complaining about where they place the price stickers? If you think they're fast when they stick on the sticker, you will not believe how fast a person can bang down a telephone receiver and tell you where to put the sticker.

As for me, I suppose I could make better use of my time than writing about how stuck I am on the subject of the location of the stupid price stickers. But I think this is just one more way that we are denied our right to know the facts.

Should we buy something that doesn't give us all of the facts?

I didn't buy the medicine since the side effects remain a mystery. And I plan to stick to that plan.

PULL THE PLUG

My satellite TV system bit the snow (not the dust) during a recent storm.

When we get a lot of snow, our satellite dish usually fills with snow and ceases to function. My husband goes on the roof and clears the snow out of the dish. Then the TV starts right back up.

In the recent storm, cleaning out the dish did not solve the problem so we had to call for a satellite service repairman. Actually we wouldn't have had to call for help if we had been reboot-savvy.

You know what *reboot* is. It's that complicated process whereby you unplug your computer-run equipment, wait fifteen seconds or more, and then re-plug. Most of the time, so I'm told, the machine will start right up. The computer brain has had a nice little nap and awakes refreshed (another very technical computer term).

I know about pulling the plug on my computer since I have to do it so often. Its brain often needs a nap right in the middle of something I'm hurrying to finish writing.

A booklet came with my computer that gave me four options on how to shut it down when it needs to be rebooted. None of them work. They've never worked. A computer whiz told me to unplug the computer; wait about a minute, then re-plug. That works.

The computer whiz did not explain to me that this rebooting procedure would work on other machines that have computer brains. She also did not tell me which machines in my house are worked by computers.

The satellite repairman arrived at my house and within minutes was giving me a lesson on rebooting. The lesson took about ten seconds. Getting the TV going again took about twenty seconds. (There was a fifteen second wait between the act of unplugging and the procedure of re-plugging.)

As the repairman was leaving, I mentioned that it would be great if we could reboot some people. His reply was, "I sometimes wish I could reboot my girlfriend."

Think about it--Wouldn't it be great if when a person's brain is not functioning properly, we could just pull a plug and then reboot?

Many times when my computer refuses to do my bidding, it is because my brain was the one that needed rebooting first.

How about this—When someone says something that you think is foolish, just say, "You need to unplug and reboot." That's a whole lot nicer than most of the put-downs you usually hear.

But be prepared if you say this because the person may respond with, "I'm going to plug you in and boot you out." (Well, it doesn't make much more sense than what you just said.)

Personally, I plan to unplug my brain with a nice nap and then I will reboot it with a lovely dinner.

Boot Appetit!

WHO'S ONE? WHO'S TWO?

It's an odd feeling when you are told that you're neither female nor male. It wasn't even a doctor who passed along this information to me.

When my pharmacist tried to activate my new Medicare-Blue Cross Blue Shield discount card, I was rejected. The pharmacist telephoned me with the news that I was turned down for "lack of gender." (Say what?)

Since I have lived long enough to be certain that I am a female, and my Medicare card states in all caps FEMALE, this situation was a big puzzle. And trying to find the answer was a big pain in the neck.

My pharmacist and I made multiple phone calls to the insurer and Blue Cross (not one and the same), Medicare and Social Security (not one and the same). Finally, we discovered that the problem all boiled down to whether or not I am number one or number two.

So what the heck did this mean? It meant that the insurer considered men to be number one. So, consequently, women are number two. Does this surprise you?

However, my pharmacist, who is a woman, told me that she feels women should be number one. Therefore, she put the number one into the little box where the insurer asked for my gender.

In a matter of seconds, I went from female to male as far as the insurer's computer was concerned. However, moments before, the insurer had seen that I am female.

This question of "Is she male or female?" could have been solved in a minute if the insurer had been allowed to tell my trusted pharmacist about the secret of the boxes. But because of our current strict Privacy Laws, the pharmacist was not permitted to discuss this delicate gender issue with anyone else except me.

The pharmacist was told only that the customer needs to call Social Security. Then Social Security said to call Medicare. Then Medicare said to call the insurer.

This is all true. Truly.

In about one minute after talking to someone at the insurer's office, the problem was solved. All that remained was to call the pharmacist who had to call the insurer to change the answer to the question in the little gender box to number two instead of one. No, the insurer would not change it when I told them I am a number two, even though they had insisted previously that they couldn't take the word of the pharmacist.

Now the pharmacist had to call to tell them my gender. Suddenly, she was to be trusted. Does this make any sense at all?

I wonder why a number had to be inserted in the box on the computer in the first place. Why didn't the insurer ask the pharmacist to put an F or an M in the box? The woman I spoke to at the insurer's office said, "Make sure the pharmacist puts a number two and not an F in the box. A lot of people do that and it won't work." (Then why didn't they change the process?)

She said this to me after she told me that I had to have the pharmacist call her. Was it a privacy issue that she couldn't pass that information along to the pharmacist?

By now, you are probably as confused as I was about this gender situation.

A good marker of where society thinks the male rates in relationship to the female is a Social Security number. Whenever a request is made for a Social Security number, it will be for the husband's number, if there is a man around the house. Little wifie's number is irrelevant.

Trust me, after more than fifty years of marriage, I know. I've been asked for my husband's Social Security number so many times that I have it memorized. I do not have mine memorized. When someone does ask me, I get so excited, I can't even think where the number is written down.

This male-is-first thing starts at or before birth. People get so excited when a boy is born. On the other hand, the reaction to the birth of a girl is less enthusiastic than when a puppy joins a household. And I'm talking about in the United States, not just some far off country overseas.

There's nothing new about this female/male issue. In fact, how much has changed for the average woman and man over the past twenty years, for example, when it comes to equality and status?

I imagine the answer is a very personal one depending on what is important to you.

Frankly, being a woman has never stopped me from doing and being what I want. But maybe I don't set my sights too high.

When all is said and done, I wouldn't trade being a woman for being a man.

However, I wouldn't mind being number one instead of number two if my gender has to go into a box. But at least I'm no longer gender-less.

THE LADIES' ROOM

There have been lots of jokes about toilets and there are even jokey books with bathroom humor, but sometimes experiences with toilets just tick me off. No joke.

I started thinking about ladies' restrooms while visiting for three days in a hospital because my husband had hip replacement. There was a bathroom within his room but of course visitors are not allowed to use it.

I had not seen a sign anywhere that indicated "restroom" so I asked a nurse where one was located. The nearest one was down a very long hall, turn right, go down a lightly shorter hall, turn right, go past the elevators and it is on your left. I had to make sure I wasn't in a rush.

Now this restroom is located on a floor that is just for orthopedic patients so you know that most of the patients are elderly, which means that the spouse probably is, too. The toilets in this particular ladies' room were very low to the ground. No toilet seat covers were provided. In a hospital where every two feet there was an antibiotic hand cleaner station, there were no toilet seat covers. Do you really want to plant your naked butt on a toilet seat where who knows who has just planted her naked butt"?

Unless you are a very mature woman you may not understand the significance of the toilet being low and there being no seat covers. The problem is, my younger friends, that older knees do not like the squatting position where you can do your duty without any part of your body touching the toilet. In fact, with a low toilet even after you have spread paper all over the seat and you have happily sat down, you may never rise again without a handrail.

Is there any question about who designed this room? Do men always have to sit when they have to "go?" Of course not. And a woman would certainly have designed the room to have a purse hanger in the stall, which this one did not include.

There were dozens of patients' rooms in the area of this tiny bathroom that had one squished up stall and one handicapped stall. The second time I went to that room the handicapped toilet was stopped up. The other stall had no toilet paper. This is a major hospital and except for this situation and the fact that the food was horrible, we had no complaints. In fact, we felt that the rest of the care was superior, so who was in charge of bathroom maintenance?

The day that the toilet was stopped up and the other one had no paper; there was a hospital staff person in there washing her hands. I said, "Did you see that the handicapped toilet is stopped up?" She said she did not. I asked her if she could report it and she said she would. I said, "What department is responsible for taking care of the restrooms?" She stated that she had no idea. So, I held out no hope that the toilet would get repaired, but to my delight, the next time I went there, all was in order.

Something about shopping in my local supermarket causes me to have to make a pit stop quite often. Maybe it's the florescent lights. They get blamed for a lot of other horrible things. Anyway, on the back of the enter/exit door, there is always a chart that shows when the room has been serviced. There's a place for the date and an initial. It always looks right up to date.

However, the bathroom does not. At least one of the three stalls always has not been flushed. Toilet paper is always decorating the floor. The hand towels are attractively strewn around the wastebasket on the floor. Let's not discuss the condition of the two sinks. But to my great surprise, there are toilet seat covers and the container is usually full. There used to be hooks on the back of the doors but they've been missing for years. The screw holes remain.

One day I went in to this bathroom and it actually looked clean. I was shocked. I looked at the chart to see when it had been initialed and it was that day and this was about 9 AM so no wonder.

I talked to some of my friends before I began going off on this tangent and they all agreed with what I was thinking and all agreed that the important thing is to make sure there is sufficient toilet paper available before ever sitting down. Thank goodness I did that this morning because there were two of those gigantic rolls of paper in a holder where you have to reach up to spin the roll to find the end. Well today, the ends were still glued down. So I simply went to the other stall where there was one roll of paper. It was almost empty, but I managed.

I know you're probably thinking, "She should hear my horror story about being caught without paper." We all have one. Mine involves getting caught without and when I asked the lady in the next stall if she would hand me some, I received one square. I was too embarrassed to ask for more. I wanted to at least save face.

I've told you before, I'm not here to give advice, only to complain, but may I suggest that carrying a purse packet of tissue could be more than a nose saver. It could also be a butt saver.

FAMOUS LAST WORDS

SLIPCOVERS

I was checking out the classified ads in one of Santa Fe's free local newspapers because the ads are more fun to read than the rest of the paper. These are not Personals. These are ads for services that could probably not be found in such abundance anywhere else on earth.

I saw ads for tarot card reading, pathworking, channeled messages from an archangel, live from your center/synergy, punching bag mantras, and dog massage.

Right in the middle of these strange services, and next to yoga, Pilates, massage, acupuncture, Tai Chi, belly dancing, and meditation, it said, SLIPCOVERS," with a phone number.

SLIPCOVERS!

It struck me that slipcovers should have been the big, bold headline above all of the above.

Think about it. What are slipcovers? They are covers over old problems. Why would you cover a new problem-free sofa or chair?

Look, I'm not opposed to any of those things advertised in the classifieds. I just ask you to consider my slipcover philosophy.

If you feel absolutely fine, with no aches, pains or head problems, do you really need one of those slipcovers? If you are happy as a whatever, you don't need a punching bag mantra, do you? (By the way, how do we know Mr. Puppy wants a massage? Maybe he needs a bone, a nice petting, and a big walk.)

Now a beautiful big surgery, lots of highly chemical medications, and twenty years of pouring out your life on a therapist's couch would be more like reconstructing the sofa and chair than slipcovering it. Don't you agree?

Life is full of these big decisions. If you've gained five extra pounds, should you go for liposuction, or do a little belly dancing? See what I mean?

By the way, do you know that archangels can type? The Archangel's messages "will be presented to you, for a fee, on 4 to 5 typed pages." Really! I saw the ad.

Once I had my handwriting analyzed by mail. I received four typewritten pages back. It took that many pages to explain that I think too much about ridiculous things.

I tried self-hypnosis and all I could think about was how ridiculous the group looked trying to imagine descending in an elevator that had no lights inside. The instructor and I sat there and giggled.

I flunked the procedure.

Well, I have to go now because I have an appointment for a massage and acupuncture in half an hour. I had my facial this morning. I'm thinking about signing up for belly dancing when I get home but I don't know if I'll have time because I'm taking our dog for a massage three days a week. The Archangel's four pages to me recommended it.

FLOORED

My floor is growing hair.

"Okay," you say, "I know where she's going with this. She's got a pet that's shedding."

Right you are. I have a 90-pound, thick-haired dog, with summer just around the corner, and dog hair everywhere.

The reason I think the problem is more than the dog shedding is that ten minutes after I mop my brick tile floors, I find more chunks of hair. And the dog hadn't been back in the house.

I hear you saying, I don't want to read another thing about someone's pet.

Well, don't worry; this isn't about pets, I promise. This is about floors.

"Oh, right, that sounds positively fascinating, you may be thinking."

When I saw the huge yellow hunk of Golden Retriever hair bunched up on my floor, which is red, I thought, if this was blonde carpeting, the hair might not show.

I live in Santa Fe, New Mexico, where nearly everyone has floors made of big square tiles. Most of the houses have brown or tan floor tiles. Tan, brown or yellow dog hair would blend in. But my house has glazed brick tiles, the reddish color of sunsets. My dog doesn't have red hair and I've never seen a red dog, except Clifford.

(If you are wondering about Clifford, you don't have young children who like books about giant dogs.)

I promised you that I wasn't going to talk about dogs, but rather about floors.

Before my husband and I moved here permanently and into a house, we bought a condo. There was carpeting throughout. Well that wouldn't do because we wanted the Santa Fe look. So we decided to tile the floor on the lower level. (There was not a dog then.)

Choosing the color of the tile became a vocation, an occupation, a job. The search was on and it ended in a hotel. The tile was in the ladies' bathroom and convincing our male contractor to go in there to see the size and color was not easy. He wondered if the men's bathroom had the same tile. No!

Later when we decided on wall tile for our bathroom, the poor man had to visit a ladies' room in yet another hotel. He must have thought that I spend a lot of time in hotel bathrooms. The truth is, I do.

Actually, I love looking at bathrooms in great hotels and restaurants. I know I'm not the only one who feels this way because one of the publications in Los Angeles came out with a big article on the best bathrooms in the city. This was a number of years ago when we still lived in LA. Anyway, I was so excited because they rated the bathrooms and my all-time favorite bathroom rated number one. The floor in that bathroom is gorgeous Italian marble. The hotel is in Beverly Hills. Where else would it be?

My carpet grew waves recently. It's true. I've had the carpet in my bedroom for ten years and a few months ago it started to pucker. I know it grew because the carpet man had to cut pieces out of it to get it to lay flat again. Carpet is made out of fabric just like our clothes, so I'm confused.

Why did the carpet grow? Do your clothes grow? Mine always seem to get tighter, not looser. Don't say it. I know what you're thinking--She's eating too many chocolate chip cookies again.

Speaking of pets, which I know I told you I wouldn't do, carpets and pets are a bad combination. I've always had cats and dogs and I've always had carpets in some rooms of my house. Carpet cleaners usually have my address and phone number memorized. I also have theirs memorized.

I have white carpet in my living room, and my dog is not allowed in there. He only goes in there when he's sick so that I won't overlook what he is leaving on the floor.

Recently, the carpet cleaner person was at my house every morning at eight o'clock for two weeks. It's true. The dog had visited the living room and the first time they cleaned the carpet, it turned red. It took fourteen additional visits to get the red out. Clifford, the big red dog, would have fit in nicely at that time.

I love pets. I love tile floors. I love quiet, soft carpets, too. I must tell you, however, I don't understand about hair growing on my tile, blonde carpets turning red when cleaned, or waves suddenly forming in my carpet.

This whole floor thing just has me floored.

THE LITTLE WOMAN

My calendar says it's 2011, but I'd swear it's 1950. I'm standing in my kitchen, wearing an apron. (You'd think I was in an episode of "Father Knows Best.") I'm trying to fix dinner. The phone is ringing for the seventh time in the last fifteen or twenty minutes.

"Is Mr. Finley there?" the sweet little female voice pours like syrup out of the phone.

When I answered the phone, I had to wait longer than a normal call to hear, "May I speak to Mr. Finley?" In the background were a lot of indecipherable sounds. The pause was a dead giveaway, so I am absolutely certain it's a marketing call.

I was annoyed on call number one. I was ticked off on number two. I was irate on number three. At number four I became furious and by number seven, I am screaming, raging, furious, over the moon, out of my mind.

Not only are they (whoever) disrupting my incredible gourmet meal that I am preparing of pre-cooked ham slices, mushrooms out of a bottle, shredded cheese from a plastic bag that you can't open or close, and REAL eggs, but they have asked for Mister Finley, not for me.

Never do they ask for the little woman of the house. Never. Surely this must be 1950 when the female married person was relegated to making decisions only about when to cook, launder and sweep the floor.

NO, NO, NO, he is not here, I shout as he stands right next to me asking, "Who is it?"

Do I call these people during their dinner or after their dinner hour or during their lunch or just before nine P.M. when their do-not-call curfew kicks in? I do not.

My big question is would these pesky marketers keep aggravating other people if they didn't enjoy some success?

My answer is no, they would not.

So my next question is, who are these people who actually respond to marketing telephone calls? Do they buy the service? Do they buy siding for their house, and magazines, and telephone services over the telephone?

Isn't it bad enough that we can't drive down the highways without being besieged with billboards? Isn't it enough that we can't watch how the world came into being on television without ads for bladder control pills? (Do you think I make this stuff up?) Are our wastebaskets big enough to hold all of the junk mail we pitch everyday? (Believe it or not, I spent twenty years as an advertising copywriter. Go figure!)

A friend of mine is always very polite to these blankity-blank people on the phone and tells them how much he enjoyed their call. Then he asks for their phone number. When they refuse, he says something on the order of, "But you called me right in the middle of my dinner, so why can't I return the favor?" The caller usually hangs up on him instead of vice versa.

Lots of us have our little scenarios that we enact when we get one of these solicitors on the phone. I have been known to say, "Just a minute." when they ask for my husband. I then set the phone down with a towel on top of it and return twenty or thirty minutes later. I wonder how long the salesman waits before hanging up.

The thing that really ticks me off is that they ask for my husband. If you are a married lady, you're probably like me--You don't know your own Social Security number, but you know your husband's by heart. Why? Because no matter what you are doing, if a Social Security number is needed, the request is for your husband's.

Just the other day, my husband and I were at the Department of Motor Vehicles and the lady clerk asked for his Social Security number. (We were both getting new licenses.) While he's digging around in his wallet, I'm reciting it to her from memory. I asked, "Do you need my number? She said, "No." I said, "Good, because I would have to look it up."

The marketing people would be very smart if they called one day and asked for Missus Finley. I would be so shocked that I'd probably end up buying subscriptions to Finance.com, or golf whatever. Both would end up in the wastebasket unread. But how thrilling to think of myself as a person and not a thing in an apron who answers the phone in order to round up my husband to come and hear about metal siding for our adobe home.

I have one very big wish when I blow out the Birthday candles on my cake or toss a penny in a wishing well. I just hope that the people who call us get called seven times every night when they are fixing dinner. Of course, that won't happen because they don't fix dinner at dinnertime. They call us instead.

SNOW AND BLOW

"Huge snowstorm to impact all of New Mexico beginning tonight through tomorrow with high winds and freezing temperatures. Snow up to 6 inches."

I woke up in Santa Fe the next morning with no new snow on the ground, not a breeze stirring, and it didn't seem all that cold.

These were important issues because my husband had an after-surgery appointment fifty miles from our home, in Albuquerque at 1:10. This meant we would have to leave by 11AM.

Checking the weather on line and TV, the report was "Huge snowstorm to…" It is now 10:15 and there is no snow, wind and the sun seems to be trying to break through.

I realize that keeping the public informed about coming weather attractions is called "predictions" and not "science" and that certainly seems to be correct.

I told my husband this morning that Mother Nature must be laughing her ass off. She is always fooling us and playing us for fools.

Why fools?

Well, I was just reading about the record high winds in California that caused multi-millions of people to be without electricity. The utility people were out in force handing out flashlights to millions of people.

I wondered, aloud, what kind of fools those recipients of the lights might be. I lived in Los Angeles for years and if you did so, you realized that earthquakes happen a lot and when they do, you are often without electricity and gas.

One Christmas, my kids asked me what I wanted for a gift and I said, "Flashlights." That is an item that seems to disappear as fast as socks in a washing machine.

So, for Christmas, I received about ten flashlights in many different sizes. Several weeks later, we had a very strong earthquake and I was doling out flashlights to my family.

Many long years ago, farmers and a lot of other people used a paperback book, The Farmer's Almanac, to figure out what the weather might be. They also used common sense and kept a history of past years in their minds about storms and droughts.

My father, who lived in a city, Tulsa, Oklahoma, would look at the sky and say, "There's a tornado on the way," because the sky would get a grey-greenish color. When the sky looked pink at night, he would tell us that we were going to get snow. He was always right.

We think we are so doggone smart because we have fancy weather reports streaming all the time on the TV and our computers but the truth is that they don't seem to be much more accurate than wetting a finger, sticking it up in the wind to see which way it's blowing.

It's no wonder that weather is the second subject we talk about with other people after "How are you?" And most of the time, we are a lot more interested in the weather than whether or not the other guy has painful knees.

That, painful body parts, is also a way many people used to, and some still do, predict the weather. If they hurt, they think either rain or cold weather is approaching. That's probably about as accurate as your local weather report.

By now, weather gurus are cursing me, I'm sure. Well, let me soothe a few ruffled feathers by complimenting those who let us know where hurricanes are going to land. However, I have to take away a little of that glory by saying that those big storms are very ponderous, moving so slowly, unlike tornadoes, and therefore brave airplane pilots can fly right into the eye and see what's happening up close and personal.

It is about fifteen minutes until the time when my husband and I would be taking off for his doctor's appointment if we hadn't cancelled. Now I'm feeling like a fool for believing the so-called weather experts. There's no snow or wind.

I have to hurry and finish this rant because if it begins to snow and blow, my whole concept will seem like a snow job and then you'll blow me off.

BUMP HUMP LUMP

When I was a kid, our streets didn't have artificially made bumps and humps. We had ordinary sunken places. Potholes.

When I was a kid, a hump was that thing on the back of Quasimodo (The Hunchback of Notre Dame). Humps were the shape on the backs of witches, who flew through the air on broomsticks, not bouncing down a road.

I teach reading to little kids. One way I instruct them is by using word groups. For example, ump is part of the words bump, hump and also lump, dump, jump, rump and pump. Pump doesn't fit into the subject of protrusions on the road, but the other words sure do.

If you hit a bump or hump going too fast in your vehicle, it will jump (up), tump (over) and dump (you upside down).

Even going slowly over those man-made hills, your rump will know you've hit a bump or hump.

Time to define the words bump, hump and lump.

A bump, the dictionary states, is a slight swelling or lump. There is nothing "slight" about something that jars the teeth out of your head.

A lump is defined as an irregularly shaped mass. Road lumps are regularly shaped and meant to shake the stuffing out of you if you exceed the speed, or even if you adhere to it.

A hump is a "rounded protuberance," defined as a swelling or bulge, by the dictionary. Try driving over the hump of a camel. Same thing.

Speaking of bulges—it's a "protruding part; an outward curve or swelling."

Now we're going around in circles--traffic circles. Just as you are careening off of one of the rump-bumping irritations on the road, you'll have to turn quickly into the tightest U-turn you've ever made. Passengers scream as if on a rollercoaster. It is a thrill ride.

But back to bump and hump. What's the difference? After devoting much thought, I have decided that a bump is more jarring than a hump.

By the way, why don't the City Fathers just leave the potholes? They slow traffic just as efficiently and cost a whole lot less than artificial bumps and humps.

On the other hand, we could avoid the streets entirely. All we have to do is just fly around on our broomsticks.

IT'S TOO LATE

I sincerely hope you are not one of those people who are perpetually late to every event because that just ticks me off.

There is the action of something some New Yorker probably named, namely "fashionably late." But most times when the always-late people are late, it is just plain unfashionably rude.

I love the excuse, "There was so much traffic." Except for a rare accident here and there, the flow of traffic is usually pretty much the same. My husband and I used to have an occasional dinner with a man who was always at least twenty minutes late, if not more. He had driven the same route hundreds of times as the restaurant was near his office so he knew what the traffic would be like. He was not fighting the jam-ups on the San Diego Freeway for Pete's sake. He was driving in quiet little Santa Fe.

I had wondered why I was so careful to always be on time, if not often early, until I took a short seniors' bus trip with my mother. She woke me every morning at 5 AM to meet the group at 8 AM. She was the first one to every event, with me in tow. When I was a kid, I was most likely at the door of my school before it was unlocked. No wonder I always cried when it rained and didn't want to go. A wet head will do that to you.

There are certain kinds of events where I think being late is especially rude: A dinner party in a home (especially in mine), a movie (especially if you are a seven-foot tall basketball player), a class (especially mine), a lecture (if you have to sit on the front row to hear), a bus tour (for which it seems at least 50% of the passengers are always late), and on and on.

When I travel on an airplane, I sit in the middle seat as my husband sits on the aisle where there is more room for his long legs. Most people who get on the plane after we do are not interested in climbing over two people to get to the window seat. And of course we are always on first or close to it. When a plane is not crowded, that means I have an empty seat next to me. However, in 2011, most airplanes fly full. So I smile at all the small women trying to get them to sit next to me. It often works but other times I end up with the biggest man on the plane who was, naturally, the last to board. This is not an exaggeration.

My dad was an on-time guy. He was raised in a railroad town. He never worked for the railroads but he loved trains and kept up with their schedules. He would take out his pocket watch, look at the train whizzing by wherever we traveled and say, "There goes the old one ten (or whatever) and it's right on time." He valued that.

There's another action, actually a non-action that never happened in the "good ole days." This involves not just being late but also not answering an RSVP. If you've given a party lately that includes more than just trusted friends, you have probably experienced this behavior. People ignore the RSVP and just show up. Really, what's worse than not saying you'll come and then arriving late?

I married a man who gets everywhere on time, by the skin of his teeth. When we first married, I nagged him to leave early and when we would get to the house where a party was being held, he'd drive around the block a bunch of times so that we wouldn't be the first ones there. I tried to leap out of the car but it was always going too fast. After almost 60 years of living with him, he now often gets ready early and I don't have a seizure because we may be two minutes late. However, we are rarely late.

What I find most interesting about the word late is when I see an obituary that mentions "the late Mr. So and So." Why isn't it the "early Mr. So and So?" I'm pretty sure the man would tell us, if he were alive, that he died before he wanted to pass on, so he went too early, not too late.

Well, it's getting late and the one thing I am usually late for is getting to bed. "Early to bed, early to rise makes a man healthy, wealthy and wise." Obviously I'm a little late in following that rule.

SQUEEZE PLAY

I've always thought of train travel as elegant and romantic. This is the way travelling by train usually appeared in the movies I saw in my youth (long ago).

The women in those movies wore fancy gloves and hats covered with flowers or feathers. The men were in starched white shirts, suits and ties.

The train compartments of old were large and decorated with red plush seats and polished wood trims.

In dining cars couples were allowed to sit across from one another during their meal so they could gaze with longing into each other's eyes.

The train my husband and I travel on every two or three months from Lamy, New Mexico to Los Angeles is not like that.

On our train, whether riding in Coach, Economy compartment, or a Deluxe room, people are dressed in jeans, polyester pants or shorts. There are certainly no women in white gloves or men wearing ties.

Everything is squeezed down on the train we take. We go in the Economy compartment so we'll have a bed on our overnight trip. Putting the two facing seats together makes up the lower bed. That's the best bed. The upper bed is a pull-down bunk and once my husband gets into it, he can't move even though he's an average size man. (He kindly sleeps above because he's afraid I would fall out even though the bunk comes complete with straps to hold you in.) There's no chance he could fall out, as he's in there tight as a sardine in a can. (An old cliché!)

The Deluxe is a bit bigger than the Economy, but the advantage, in my opinion, is a private bathroom. The disadvantage is the Deluxe costs about twice as much as the Economy, which is more than the Coach. Another disadvantage is that even though the bathroom is private, it is just large enough to hold a toilet with a showerhead over it. If you want to shower, you must sit on the lid of the toilet. This does not spell Deluxe to me.

Unless the train is practically empty, you will not get to gaze into your significant others' eyes in the dining room. You'll be squashed intimately shoulder to shoulder while gazing into the eyes of two strangers. Maybe it's best to travel with two other people you know and like.

The corridors to get from the tiny bedrooms to the teeny shared bathrooms and to the small dining tables require that you stagger along in single file. It's not a drunk thing. It's a rough-train-track thing. And the sad part is that train tracks don't have to be rough. High-speed trains in Europe are smooth as silk. I think it's a money thing. A railroad-saving-money thing.

One positive is that it will take you a lot longer by train to get to where you are going than if you went on an airplane. This probably sounds odd, but when you have all that time, you can get in lots of naps (which you'll need because sleeping at night on a lurching train with freight trains swishing past your window all night long takes getting used to), and you can finish an entire novel.

If you carry along your own DVD player as we do, you'll be able to see the movies you want to see, in massively reduced size. Then there's the old fashioned activity of talking to each other without the loud drone of jet engines in your ears. For some couples, conversing might be a negative.

The modern train we travel on may not be like the luxurious trains of movie history, but I love travelling by train (surprise!) and would choose it over any other mode of transportation, except a cruise ship sailing around the Greek Islands.

When you travel by train in the United States, you do have to squeeze into the miniature facilities, but on the other hand, you'll have a huge amount of time to play.

In fact, my definition of travelling by train is, it's the ole "squeeze play."

LINES IN MIND

I've got lines on my mind. No, this is not a song title.

I started thinking about lines the first day I had to take my new car to the dealer's for service. I arrived before the garage opened and parked behind the car that was nosed up to the door.

To me, that meant that I was second in line.

In the fifty years I had been driving and taking my car in for service, but not to this place, I have always had a service person come up to me at my car to take the necessary information. So I stood beside my car for several minutes. Finally another customer said, "You have to go into the office to check in."

There was one person at each of the two (out of five) functioning counters but everyone else in the room was hither, thither and yon. Mostly yon. I didn't know where to stand without offending someone. Before I had to make a move, one person left a counter and the service person said, "Who was next in line with a car?"

Whew! Me! Me! Me!

Not knowing where to stand presented a real problem to me because, where I live now, very few people seem to understand the concept of standing toe to heel, one behind the other, to form a line. Apparently only those of us who arrived from bigger cities know the rules of how to stand in line for service.

This car service event was what first got me interested in lines.

The second event boosted the first one and sent me flying off on this missive. Not on a missile.

The same day, in the afternoon, I watched a car in front of me weaving its way down the highway, crossing back and forth over the lines marking the lanes. I said to my husband, as I pointed ahead, "That driver didn't learn to color between the lines in Kindergarten."

By the time I got home, all I could think about were lines, so I looked up the word in the dictionary. There were nineteen definitions of the word line. Amazing, I thought.

I recalled what I had said about coloring between the lines in Kindergarten and realized that children learn to read and write by making lines. Think about it. You can't read if you don't know the alphabet. I teach beginning young readers. When we work on the alphabet, I say, "Now, children, you make an A by drawing lines like this." I demonstrate. For my efforts, I receive wide eyes and blank looks.

Think about how many lines a day children will have to make if they are printing the letters of the alphabet over and over. And it must be very confusing to learn that the word line means a mark on paper as well as what kids stand in to get their lunch.

Speaking of lines for lunch, my Little Sister, who just started her first year of Middle School, was having difficulty getting her lunch in time to eat it without being late for her next class. And believe me, she can eat fast.

This young, hungry girl brought the problem to the attention of the school authorities. They attempted to find a solution by making two lines instead of only one very long line. They continued, however, to have only one cashier, so nothing changed.

Duh! As my Little Sister would say.

What must a child think when a frustrated mother says, "Now you've stepped over the line." Frantically the child might look for a lunch line or a mark like an A on the floor.

I warned you that there are nineteen definitions of the word line in my dictionary.

I'll get to another definition soon, but there is one word we use that is not defined in my dictionary. The word is Line-Cutters. These are the people who are challenged by something in their makeup to wiggle ahead of everyone else in line to get to the front.

I heard about the sport of line-cutting many years ago, but had never seen it in action until I went to obtain a visa to visit the Orient. The people from Japan, China and other Far East countries, who I saw, were Olympic champions at making their way to the front of the line without drawing blood or screams.

It took me at least twice as long as it should have to work my way to the front of the line since I stayed where I was, considering cutting in line to be rude, not heroic.

This is still my opinion.

I'm leaving out a few definitions of the word line so you can have fun thinking of your own.

Here, though, is number nineteen—In math, the word line means the path of a moving point.

Not being mathematically inclined, I have no idea what that definition means, but otherwise I could probably keep right on about points having to do with lines.

I hope you get my point.

If not, I'm sorry as this is the end of the line for now.

BOO BOO SHOES

Is there anyone who gets through life without experiencing confrontation? I grew up with the expert in avoiding confrontation but she was not 100%. Well, that was mainly because I'm her daughter and most of her experience with confrontation was with me.

The climate I grew up in required snowsuits in the winter. We called them that in the 1930's. We also liked to wear warm slippers, which people then called house shoes. That is, everyone except my mother called them that. She called them "boo boo shoes." No, I am not making this up.

One Christmas, she received some slippers as a gift. They were too big but she was going to wear them with heavy socks so she wouldn't have to return them to the store. Anything to avoid a confrontation. I managed to convince her that she should take them back and told her that I would go with her for support.

When we got to the store, she nervously handed the clerk the box and said, "These boo boo shoes are too big for me." I was choking back a laugh but my mother's best friend was also with us and hee-hawing like a horse. Meantime, my poor embarrassed mother was turning beet red, as the clerk had no idea what she was talking about.

I think of my mother when I get on the telephone with some utility company who has screwed up my service or my bill. You know the drill: Punch this number, punch that number and when you've completed that series you sigh happily before the robot woman (It's hardly ever a man.) tells you that you get to choose between several other numbers. Oh, goody!

Now you have arrived at your destination but not with a live person. If you are lucky enough that you didn't have to listen to some terrible music, then every few minutes another robot lady will interrupt your reading or writing to tell you that you absolutely must not hang up because someone will be with you "shortly." Excuse me, what is the definition of "shortly?" The answer is anywhere from one to twenty minutes, if you're lucky.

Finally we are to the point of confrontation if you have been able to follow the punch-the-correct-number instructions, which my mother couldn't do even before she went to the senior facility.

Confrontation seems to be an integral part of having repairs done to your house.

For example, the first thing that happens when water is running down your hallway from the bathroom is that the person answering the phone at the plumber's tells you that they might be able to fit you in next week. Now if that's Friday, that's not even a choice. If you win the argument, they'll be at your house between 9 and 12 tomorrow, for an overtime charge, but won't tell you more than that. "Okay, so we'll call you before we come" is the best you can hope for.

You get up at 8:30 the next morning even though you like to sleep until 9:30 on Saturday. You get dressed, etc., and at five minutes to twelve, the plumber calls and says he had an emergency (like you don't) and so he'll be there between 1 and 4, but he'll call you before he comes, like that makes it okay. Never mind that you've waited for an appointment for two months to get your hair cut and colored at 3 o'clock that very afternoon.

Now you're wondering if you can get your husband to come home early from his regular Saturday golf game. Probably not an option. Maybe your mother, who no longer is allowed to drive, could take the bus over to cover for you. After all, she only has to change busses twice and she can ride in her wheelchair for heaven sake. Probably not an option. Time to cancel the beautician.

So, you know the script—The plumber arrives at five minutes to four but he doesn't have the right equipment to fix the problem and tomorrow is Sunday so he'll just stop the water by turning it off to the entire house and he'll see you between 9 and 12 on Monday. He'll call before he comes.

This is the point where you do NOT have a confrontation. You know you're not going to win and if you tick off the plumber, you'll have to start this whole process over with some other company. All you do is thank him profusely for arriving so promptly at your house when you know he must be up to his eyebrows in water problems. Just tell him, "Have a cookie. I baked them while waiting for you from 9 this morning to 4 this afternoon."

But really, we can't avoid confrontation. There's only one thing we can do and that's to confront it. I just hope you're not going to argue with me about that.

GIVE IT A GO

Loud clanks and muted curses are rolling on the sound waves out of our laundry room where we more or less maintain a tool drawer. I say more or less because there is no, none, nada organization in the drawer.

My husband is in there attempting to open a new bottle of liquid dishwashing soap. The bottle designer at the bottling company must have visualized this products' use by women descendants of Jane of the jungle. I am not your 90-pound weakling but I could not open the bottle even with rubber gloves or banging on the counter, all of which are women's tools, as I'm sure you (women) know. And no man is going to be reading something like this unless it is about football, beer or naked women.

Wow, here comes my man who can kill bear with his bare hands, or so he indicated to me when he went off to the laundry jungle to deal with the soap bottle. He's holding the bottle above his head, screaming, "I've conquered it!" and running in place like Rocky at the top of the steps after his winning fight in the ring.

"My hero," I say, clapping my hands, trying to show my tremendous joy.

What is it about the new bottles of virtually everything? They really should be sold with their own opening tools. "Push in while twisting" to open a bottle with a cap that I can barely put my hand around, and believe me, I have extra long fingers. That was what it said on the soap bottle and even my 6 foot 1 inch husband couldn't turn the monster.

One of my grandsons was in the kitchen on a day I was attempting to open a new bottle of salad dressing. I got the cap off with no problem. What comes next is a joke. It is one of those papers glued down to the rim of the hole. It had an extra half of a paper glued to that. The idea is to lift up the half paper, pull and voila! The paper below comes right up. When? When does that really happen? Never, in my case. So you try using your newly manicured thumbnail to pry the paper off of the rim. This glue is what they use to put together the parts of the rockets that go to outer space.

So I'm standing there muttering madly to myself, choking down the curse word that keeps trying to bubble up when my six-year-old grandson asks me what's the matter. I tell him what I'm trying to do and he says, "Oh, Grandma, you need a man around the house. I'll open it for you." And by the way, granddad is in the next room. Evidently my grandson has seen his granddad in the past working to open a bottle.

I hand the bottle to my tiny-for-his-age grandson who proceeds to pull the seal right off of the bottle and I say, "How do you do that?" His helpful answer is, of course, "I don't know; it's easy."

In a few minutes, I go into the other room and tell granddad what just happened and his reply is, "Sure, but he can't open a bottle of liquid dishwashing soap."

My bet is that my grandson could probably do that as well and I plan to let him give it a go next time I "need a man around the house."

APOLOGIES

I read a lot of Thrillers and Mysteries and those books always have a page thanking all of the policemen and lawyers and coroners who gave the author expert information for their stories.

I would like to thank all of the people who have ticked me off (because they provided me with the material for this book), but that's probably not appropriate, so I'll stick with apologizing.

However, I am not apologizing to the people who ticked me off. I'm apologizing to all of the wonderful plumbers, electrician, roofers, security people, auto repair people, etc. whom I work with now after having been ticked off by the ones before them. That's the great thing about being ticked off, it pushes you to solve the problem and end up with very few annoyances in your life.

Frankly, I had to stop writing my ticked off pieces because I've run out of things that tick me off so don't look for a sequel to "Ticked Off and Tickled About It." I'm sure that really ticks you off.

Lou Finley's background reads like someone who can't commit. She was an advertising copywriter, residential real estate broker, owner of Two Bears Gallery in southern California, an originator of an after-school program at the Boys and Girls Club in Santa Fe, New Mexico, where she lives, a Big Sister with the Big Brother/Big Sister organization, a writer of many odds and ends, and the author of a children's book "How To Do Nothin'." She is also a wife of fifty years (Oh, so she can commit!), a mother, a mother-in-law, a grandmother of two boys, a pet adopter of a big dog and two small cats. And hopefully, a good friend.

My blog site "Tea With the Tickled Lady" is at ---www.tickedoffandtickled.com

Website for "How To Do Nothin'" is at www.nothin-kids-book.com

This book could not have been produced without the expertise of Brian Finley, author of "Ryder's Army" an Ethan Ryder Thriller. Video trailer at www.wix.com/rydersarmy/rydersarmy

TICKED OFF
2012

13 Houses Publishing

This book is based on true events but there's exaggeration and some humorous made-up stuff Nobody who ticked me off is named. You can breathe easy.

ISBN: 0615589480
ISBN-13: 978-0615589480

Cover designed by: Budow Design
www.budowdesign.com